SAY MY NAME

BY

CHRISTINE WREN

Say My Name by Christine Wren

ISBN: 978-0-6455379-4-9 (Paperback)
ISBN: 978-0-6455379-5-6 (eBook)

Any references to historical events, real people, or real places are used fictitiously. Names, characters, and places are products of the author's imagination.

Cover image: public domain background image from pxhere.com 836631. Wasp purchased from iStock - epantha 138023535.
Typeset and cover design: Ben Morton

This book is to celebrate all of us
who have survived domestic abuse,
and lived to tell the story.

Thanks to God, my Guide

Thanks to my precious treasures: My Little Love, my fabulous kids Bec, Josh and Adam, and my friends – you all know who you are. You all encouraged me in your own way.

Thanks to my editors – Sue Pearson who persevered with me at the beginning of the process with patience and grace, and to Gabi Plumm (Inst. Of Prof. Editors.) who completed the task with kindness and amazingness, which pushed me over the finish line.

Thanks to Ben Morton (Immortalise) for meticulous formatting and preparation for publishing as well as my fabulous cover design, along with other insightful elements.

Thanks to my Book Club friends, who became Beta Readers with constructive feedback and great company on a Sunday arvie.

Poem: Beyond You

(From *Love and Other Comforts* by Chris Wren)

I am becoming myself
Keep completely still and you may find me
Layers off
Ripped by fire and wind
Skinned bone now
In my space not yours
Not theirs
Snatching pieces back like toys you stole
Words scramble for attention
Archived
Downwardly spiralling
Keeping still
My great discipline
Silence now mine
See you
Rapping on my glass house
Marbled with friction and fracture
Safe from sound
Eyes closed
Blacking you out at last

PROLOGUE

Jennifer Slade 1950s

My school holidays start in six days. That's actually less than a week. Can't wait. It's already lazy, hazy stinky hot. Cicadas are buzzing my head off. My teacher said the noise is them rubbing their legs together. Glad they're not human size. I laugh at the crazy idea.

I'm on my rickety front fence rocking. In my very best pink organdie dress and black patents. I'm doing my rhyming. Mum calls it "rhyming slang." She taught me. She's English and doesn't really like it here.

"Apples and pears: stairs; frog and toad: road; rubbedy-dub: pub."

Sometimes I make up my own. Like pats and rats: cats. Rice and dice: mice. Mine aren't as good as the others.

My sister, Fiona is about somewhere. I can hear her.

'Jenny! Where are you, Jenny?'

I'm waiting for Mum to come.

She came by last week and stayed a few days. Dad went out when she walked in. That left me and Fiona who is two years younger. Only eight.

'Just us girls together.' Mum smiled, glancing round the kitchen, putting things away in the cupboards.

I think I'm the favourite. Well, for a start, I'm the oldest. Surely that counts. So when I was in bed late one night — and when she's here — Mum lets us stay up 'til whenever we like. She came into the bedroom I share with Fiona. Fiona was asleep, I think.

Mum sat down on the edge of my bed which gave out a squeak. She lay down next to me with her head on the pillow. I love her wavy brown hair. She smells sort of perfume-y like the violets in the garden. And something else as well a bit sour. 'Shhh. I've got a surprise.' I sprang up straight away, all sleep forgotten. She glanced over at Fiona, spread out over the top of her red chenille bedspread like a dead person. Or how I think a dead person would be.

'You and I are going to the ballet. Swan Lake is coming to town. It's the Sydney production.' She jumped up and did a bit of a twirl but landed with a thump on the floor. Fiona didn't stir, she sleeps deep.

'Saturday afternoon. I've got the tickets. Just me and you.'

I jumped out of bed and joined her on the floor. I threw my face into her warm neck. I was tingling like Fruit Tingles all in my head. I hung on tight. I didn't want this moment to end. But it did. It did. I didn't want her to leave again.

'Thank you, Mummy. Thank you. But, what about...' I nodded towards my sister.

'Too young. Ssh.' And she was gone.

So I'm waiting now. It's Saturday at last. I don't know what the time is but I've been here a long time. The ballet in Sydney is today. Today!

I want to see all that frothy white tulle-y stuff the ballerinas wear. Like I've seen in the books Mum's shown me. How amazing to actually have the tickets. I waited 'til the last possible minute to get dressed in my new pink dress. I love the tiny embroidered rose-buds all over the skirt. I look like a ballerina too.

Don't be late! Please don't be late. Mummy wasn't home the night before. Not unusual these days. Daddy said she was staying with a friend and not to worry. Don't be late, Mum. Where are you? I'm beating a beat on the fence with my shiny patent shoes, bought just for the ballet.

There are long shadows across the garden. Mrs. Hallows next door is home from work. She's a hairdresser and cuts my hair sometimes. I've unravelled the pink stitching on the hem of my dress. The back of my patents is scratched from the rusty wire on the fence. My bum is completely numb from sitting so long. Somewhere in a place inside me, I'm numb too.

Fiona and the kid next door come running into the garden, chasing each other, laughing and shouting. They look over at me then take off round the house to the back yard.

No one is coming. The afternoon has gone. The sun has slipped behind the hills and the cicadas are really going for it. Dad has his comfy big arm around my shoulders. He smells of soap mixed with tobacco. It's his smell. He helps me down from the fence. My legs won't work properly. Hope I'm not in trouble for unpicking the lace edge on my new pink dress, now ragged and torn. I want my dad to pick me up. I want a cuddle.

'I don't think she's coming back, Jenny. I'm sorry darling.'

He takes my hand and we walk into the house together wrapped in a sad deep-down place. A sadness we know we share.

In bed I can't stop crying. I bite the pillow through to the kapok filling. It's happened again. But this time it's different. Something inside me is breaking.

'No longer the child of before will rule,
But a bird on the wing, reaching ascent
And so have you flown the coop'.

This time it seemed Derek had given up. As though a light had gone out on the inside. For good. He fell into the habit of leaving the back porch light on and the key in the door ... just in case.

The girls never asked.

One night Jenny heard a muffled noise from his bedroom. Was Dad crying? The loud rows had come to an end replaced by a world of nothing. A vacuum of unanswered questions. Late one night she had tiptoed out into the hallway and heard her mum talking in a pleading voice. Mummy! Jenny ran toward the kitchen, but just as she reached the closed door, she heard the crash of something heavy hitting the floor. Then shattering glass. Her mother was crying loudly. Derek's voice rose about her sobs. 'Just get on with it. I don't care anymore. It doesn't matter anymore. It's over anyway.'

A door slammed. Jenny tiptoed back to bed and lay quiet and still for a very long time.

And it was over. A sadness like an unexpected death settled on the Slade family. Derek rattled around inside the house, a grey spectral presence in a mausoleum.

Without Hermione the house was empty and a heavy fog submerged them all, making it hard to see and hard to move.

From the moment her mother left, Jenny felt the grey nothingness of invisibility which came on her in shops and school. It came too when she allowed herself to begin to actually feel instead of act. Or over-react really. The invisible thing which settled over her made her truly believe she was invisible.

The whole world continued about their business, as Jenny looked at the passing parade like some kind of movie she wasn't a part of anymore.

There was a flame of plain fury there too. Once she'd been coming out of the school gate and one of her friends asked her the forbidden question: 'Where's your mother?'

Jenny froze, searching for the right answer. She looked at the ground. 'She's away just now.' She turned and ran all the way home, hot tears coursing down her face. She had grabbed the kitchen scissors and begun cutting the tops off the flowers in her mother's garden. Lavender and rosemary buds flew in all directions. She chopped them up with a garden knife, and put them in an old teapot, then cast spells all around the house in an effort to make the family invisible too.

Derek Slade seemed to diminish and recede into nothingness. Even at his job with Evan and Evan Accountants he seemed to disappear. It was as though he vaporized and disappeared along with Hermione. Resentment trickled in like treacle in milk, colouring the family. Jenny studied hard, excelling dutifully, proving a point. On her twelfth birthday, she hoped against hope for a visit from her mum. Nothing. Not even a card.

She watched her father stirring mince and onions on the stove, adding dried herbs from a jar, while spaghetti spat steam up to the ceiling.

'Now watch this, Jen. Time you learned to cook and take over the kitchen. Well and truly.'

Jenny thought of the pile of homework waiting for her on the dining room table.

She leaned her elbows on the kitchen bench. 'How do you know when the spaghetti's ready Dad?'

He gave her a devilish smile. 'You ready?' He scooped out a couple of steaming spaghetti strands and threw them on the ceiling where they stuck.

'If they stick on the ceiling – they're ready! Go get your sister. We are ready to serve. You can do it next time.'

Jenny ran out to the yard where Fiona was playing hop-scotch with the kid next door. She hoped next time would never come.

Her sixteenth birthday rolled around.

'You're a big girl now,' her father had said, 'We don't need to have a party. It'll just be us.'

Not really a birthday at all. Derek had done his best rallying the girls. Fiona was fourteen. Between them all they ran the house in slap-dash chaos. Jenny carried a heart full of hope for a future she could only dream about. It rarely had anything to do with her dad or Fiona. Or her mum. Or even Gideon Vale.

Her final year at school had come and gone. Plunging headlong into excellence she had earned herself a scholarship to Armidale Uni and leapt at the chance. Juggling home and the kitchen, with its burned rissoles and endless spag bol she attempted to cook, and her father's grey days of disappearance had taken their toll. The Mecca café in town had given her a Saturday morning job in the kitchen too, for a bit of extra cash. She saved like crazy. A future loomed. Fiona's turn to cook and clean now.

Her dad and Fiona had stood, forlorn figures waving goodbye on the kerb as the Greyhound bus took her off into an uncertain future. She felt the tears welling up like a dam about to burst. She turned her head away from the window, surprised at the unexpectedness of them.

The first year away from home had flown by. She studied Psychology and sat spell-bound as her lecturer taught on a different way to think. Jenny had found her place in some ways with a group of girls who knew nothing of her family history. She'd studied hard but also gone to a few off-campus parties. Tasted beer for the first time. She remained an anonymous girl with no history to share. The boys she met seemed shallow and gullible. She could spin them any yarn she wanted and they believed her. Found that so easy. And freeing.

Ralph was a tall, gangly blond boy with an open face like an unread page.

'So ... is your mum missing you, Jen?' he had asked her one day over a milkshake in a local café. 'Gee, my mum misses me so much. And my brothers. And Dad too I reckon.'

'Oh yes. She sure is. I get letters every week from her. I'm loving being away though,' she lied.

At the start she'd missed home, her dad and Fiona and their simple little lives. Most of all she missed Caroline, her forever friend.

Not having a mum of her own she tended to confide a bit in Caroline's mum Celia. But only a bit.

At the end of that first year, being away from home had become normal. She loved the seasons of New England, even the starkness of winter where crunchy leaves flung themselves about and left skeleton trees standing alone.

Her first morning home, she jumped on her bike and raced off to Caroline's. So much could happen in a year. She ran in their back door and down to Caroline's bedroom. The two girls squealed together hugging and laughing. They sat shiny eyed on the bed, all smiles.

Caroline clasped her hands over her chest. 'I've got something to tell you.'

Jenny grabbed her shoulders. 'I bet I know! You've met someone?'

Caroline smiled and widened her eyes.

'Tell me everything.'

'I will, but guess what? He's got a friend who'd be perfect for you.'

'Well. That is news. What's his name?'

'Bob. Bob O'Hare. You'll really like him, Jen. He's really good looking. You know what they say – tall, dark and handsome! Just your type. Doesn't say much but I'm sure you can draw him out.' She jumped off the bed pulling Jenny up with her.

'Come on. Let's ride downtown.'

Jenny had no idea what her type was. Wow. A first date. But she trusted Caroline to know what was best for her. She allowed Caroline to set up a blind date for her and Bob. With Caroline and her new boyfriend, Geoff as well. Best be on the safe side.

Jenny had never been on a blind date before and was apprehensive to say the least. What if he's boring? What if he doesn't like her? What if ... what if?

Two men walked into the milk bar where Jenny and Caroline waited. They both looked unsure. The shorter of the two was sandy haired and freckled. His nose was peeling from sunburn. A bland face like an open field. This was surely not the tall, dark and handsome that Caroline had described. Slightly behind him was a tall, rangy man with a shock of black hair falling across his forehead. His dark eyes darted about the café like a cat looking for the way out. His arms seemed too long for the rest of him as he clenched and unclenched his hands. Jenny automatically pulled her fringe over her forehead to cover her birthmark. She lifted her head and gazed at him full in the face, feeling the first stirrings of excitement as their eyes met. A slow smile spread across Bob O'Hare's gaunt face. 'Hi,' he said, extending an arm, 'You must be Jenny.'

Geoff and Bob ordered burgers and shakes and sat down in the booth. Paul Anka prophesied loudly from the juke box. 'You Are My Destinyyyyy.'

They wandered along the Saturday afternoon streets of the town, now soaked in the warm afterglow of a summer's heat.

Bob had been shy but guarded and it was true, she had been able to draw him into conversation. They had agreed to see each other again. Later the girls sat on Jenny's front porch steps.

'Yeah. He's nice. I like him. Bit hard to talk too but I guess...'

'Give it a go, Jen. He's just quiet. First boyfriend, hey?'

It was to Caroline's mother, Celia that she confided some of her dreams about Bob. The next best thing to a real mum. Celia had not been so sure about this new man. She was British to the core, a lot like Jenny's own mum with a high expectation of her daughter, and hadn't felt comfortable with this new boyfriend of Jenny's. They sat down together at the kitchen table and Celia set out tea and Saos on the red check tablecloth.

'I mean to say, Dear, what's his educational standard? I mean to say, Dear, you're at Uni aren't you?' Her look said it all. Arched eyebrows and her ever-so-sensitive mouth pulled down at the corners. Celia was a woman who expected more from life but usually got less. She considered that she had married beneath her station but was unsure exactly what that station was.

Jenny had persevered with Bob, charmed by his occasional attentive ways, his quiet acceptance of her. Even his long silences had not bothered her much back then. The summer holidays stretched away. There were movies together, walks on the beach, double dates with Geoff and Caroline, drive-ins and just simple smooching on Jenny's front steps, often interspersed with Fiona's snooping and giggling as she followed them round at home.

'What are you thinking about, Bob?'

'Nuthin'.'

She and Caroline had laughed about it.

From Celia, with a sniff from her aristocratic nose. 'Still waters run deep, Dear. Hopefully.'

It had been over five months now and Uni went back soon. In the salty pink dusk, Jenny and Bob sat together on the sand dunes below the boulders on the edge of the Seven Mile holding hands. Jenny leaned in and kissed him lightly

'What is it? You're a thousand miles away.'

'Nuthin.'" He glanced away letting the sand sift through his fingers. 'Nuthin'. Really.'

Jenny pulled away and sprang up, hands on hips looking down at him. 'Hey. When am I going to meet your mum and the family? You said your dad's not around? We could go next weekend. Tenterfield's not that far to drive. It's close to my Uni too.'

At Jenny's mention of his mother Bob threw a fistful of sand down the beach. Everything in him clenched. How could he take this lovely unaware girl into the den of hard-eyed angry women? They'd eat her alive and that would be that. She'd judge him and find him guilty as charged. His mother was a caged tiger looking for meat, or at the least a chew on something. But he'd stalled long enough. After all, he and Jen were talking futures, kids. All that. He'd bite the bullet.

He reached up for her hand and held it. With a half-smile he said, 'OK. Let's go down this weekend. But look, Jen ... my family ... well ... they're Irish and we all grew up sort of a bit crazy.' He finished his sentence with a shudder.

Jenny gave a short yap of a laugh then quickly swallowed it. 'God, it can't be any worse than mine. Mum left me sitting on a fence waiting for her when I was a kid and I've never seen her since. Me and Fiona just brought ourselves up. Dad went AWOL. You're not Robinson Crusoe you know.' Her mouth became a long hard line. She sat down next to him and he drew her in, pulling her face gently into his chest. The wind began to gust in from the sea.

'Jen. I don't know how to say this, but ... I, I'm falling for you in a big way. I want us to be together ... well, forever really.'

She lifted her head and opened her mouth. Her kiss sank into his body like something electric exploding every dead thing inside him. A small sigh escaped him like something that had finally found home. He pulled her down on top of him, with an urgency he'd never experienced before that seemed to threaten his very life.

Jen snuggled into him stroking the dark hair off his forehead. 'I think I love you, too.'

They stayed locked in the long moment on the cold sand believing in the impossible for the first time. A sob skittered around his chest like an unfettered dog looking for an escape route. It came out as a jerky breath. A tear snaked its way down the ridge of his cheek. In some unchecked place deep inside him something like hope poked its head around the partly opened door.

At the weekend they drove to Tenterfield.

His mother met them at the door.

'This is Jenny, Mum. The girl I told you about.'

A short dumpy women stood with her hands on her hips, legs straddling the open doorway. Maureen O'Hare wiped her hands on her apron, gave Jenny a cursory glance, and with a derisive sniff, turned her back on them both clumping back to the kitchen.

Bob's two sisters, now in their late teens barely acknowledged Jenny and stayed mainly in their rooms, only coming out to sit at the kitchen table to scoff down the tasteless Shepherds' Pie that their mother had thrown together. No one spoke at the table; the silence a dead weight.

Bob cleared his throat. 'Jenny's thinking of doing her nursing now, Mum.' Jenny shot him a questioning glance. What was he talking about? Maureen leapt in before she could say anything.

She sniffed. 'Pays well does it, then? More than the likes of me's ever had, I'm betting.' His mother continued to shovel runny mince into her mouth. Bob's sisters gave each other sidelong glances and giggled.

Maureen O'Hare remained sullen, like a brewing storm, occasionally looking over at Jenny and Bob. Bob kept his eyes down, nervously tapping his knife against the cracked white plate. He fidgeted in his chair. Jenny left most of her meal on the plate, unable to take in such blatant hostility lodged in one woman.

'There's no dessert. No time.'

After lunch, Jenny jumped up to help with the dishes.

'You sit down now. You're the guest.' Maureen wheeled around to her daughters. 'And don't think the likes of you two are getting away with no dishes.' She flicked a grubby tea towel at them. 'Get to work, you lazy pair.'

Bob glanced at his watch. His face was set like a man with necessary bad news.

'Got to go, Mum. Beat the traffic. But I just need to tell you, we're going to get married. We'd love you to come.' Jenny smiled up at him but he kept his eyes on his mother.

She went to take hold of Mrs. O'Hare's hand as they were leaving. 'We would love you to come down for our wedding, wouldn't we, Bob? I, I don't have a mum anymore but my dad'll be there.'

Snatching her hand away, Maureen fished around in her apron pocket for a hanky. 'We'll see. Can't promise anything.' And she

13

turned and stomped back down the hallway to the kitchen. Jenny and Bob stood alone in the open doorway. The girls stayed in the kitchen.

They were silent in the car as they drove back to Gideon Vale until Jenny said, 'Wow, that was hard. Are they always like that?'

'Like what? That's just them. How they are. Don't expect too much.' His face was grim and he tightened his grip on the wheel.

'And what's all this about telling your mother I'm planning to do my nursing? I'm only thinking about it at the moment. We've got loads of time.' She went to ruffle his hair but he pushed her hand away.

'I don't reckon all that psychology stuff is right for a woman. The sooner you leave and start the nursing the better.'

It was a long trip back home.

The wedding was small and in the local Baptist church. Caroline was elated to be number-one bridesmaid, as was Fiona to be the other one. Bob's family decided not to come after all.'

'Not worth driving all that way,' his mother had said. Bob hid his disappointment in a few beers with the men from work.

Derek Slade walked his daughter down the aisle, the happiest she'd seen him for a long time.

Jenny had given up her Psychology degree as Bob had suggested and was happy enough studying to become a nurse. Seemed like a natural.

Bob's silences were disquieting, but life was full and busy. No regrets.

Prologue

CHAPTER 1

Bob O'Hare contained sub-surface rage like an artesian bore. Cold. No peace in it. Ragged somehow. Jenny felt its quiet terror like something alive. The scuttle of rats in the cellar.

There's quiet and then there's quiet. Not the tranquil flow of water over rock. More a flow with a source of its own. Hidden currents. Not really like anything familiar to her. The quietness of it threatened her. The measured tone. Words like bullets smashing into her makeshift armour plate. Sometimes the words rained down when she wasn't on guard and swept her away in a torrent. Firing away at the fragments of her tattered image like a scarecrow's clothes in a storm. A soldier taking pot-shots. Keeping in practice.

Nothing showed on his face that was any different to normal. Well, his normal. No giveaways. Still the smile, not a real smile mind you, just the corners of his mouth turned up as though the rest was sucking something bitter, and probably was.

A measured tone. A controlled man, Bob O'Hare. Belt and braces. A man's man.

Bob, dark skinned, dark haired, dark natured. A large man with a frame too long for conventional furniture. The gauntness of his face etched in permanent pain, the creases deepening around his long, crooked nose and his mouth setting now into permanency as middle age pursued relentlessly. The bitterness etched like acid in glass like generations before him. Jenny thought about Bob's inheritance. And now what she had inherited through the marriage. And that old security guard of guilt accompanying Bob along as he lived his life out in its desperation.

Irish ancestry. The troubles. What had gone before. And not genetically modified.

Fault lines. Ley lines. Down through the line.

She remembered the rage and chaos of Bob's mum's house — second generation Irish. The old fibro house on its stumps down near Tenterfield in NSW with the old backyard dunny.

Bob barely spoke of the past, believing, like so many, that it would die away if it was denied long enough. Like walking into a warzone. A parallel realm and unlike anything Jenny had ever known in her own life. Maureen's large white freckled face, impassive and flat, black currant eyes darting under their lids, her thin mouth set like a slashed pocket. The grim lines of resentment and bitterness from a life unfulfilled.

She had dismissed Jenny early, probably because of her English heritage, her education and her refinement. The two women were worlds apart but collided frequently. Jenny had never heard a sorry or a thankyou from this family. Another breed altogether.

Bob's memories of his early years were too dark to bring into the scrutiny of memory.

It had not been a home, but four walls encasing the fury that sometimes spilled out into the street. They were never calm or quiet. A storm waiting to happen as if it lived under the roof. By default. Like something unleashed and unstoppable. His mother, Maureen, crunching and spearing words into her husband Don's head until he exploded into murderous black attacks silencing her sometimes even with his fist.

'You and the bloody war. Time you got over all that by now.'

Quiet at last. The local priest visiting from time to time checking on his country parishioners, seeing but not saying.

And the child, Robert Patrick O'Hare, the silent witness making his vows for the future. Planning to "never" and "always".

He hid in the back shed, hands over his ears speaking the "Our Fathers" to drown out the yelling and the curses, loving and hating at the same time. Ambivalence the common ground. Longing for peace, longing for freedom and an escape to something better. The back shed. The scene of the memories that played like a dark video over and over. His sisters, sleeping three to a bed clinging together for comfort. Awash with urine in the morning, its acrid smell floating through the house. The shameful haul of wet sheets soaking in the old stone tubs in the laundry.

'So which one of yez was it last night, then?'

The only boy in the family, Robert had become the eternal scapegoat for his father's unspent rage.

The sounds. The smells. The heavy stench of rum on his father's breath on those dreaded Friday nights as he lurched in the door. And young Robert, hauled out of bed whimpering, wanting the warmth of the bed. Half asleep but the grip of fear waiting with its steel clamp.

Hauled like the whipping boy that he was, to the dark parts of the garden where the shed loomed like a familiar enemy in the waiting night, mocking his stolen innocence in a relentless pursuit that he could not evade. His dog, Scrag, barking and straining at his leash joining the noise, and as mad as the rest. Neighbours' windows slamming shut, ashamed to be witness to such behaviour but not wanting to intrude. Ever. He saw their faces in the morning, quickly averted as they walked past him pretending it was all a bad dream in the night. The shame. The fear. The quick steps getting away from the reality of the neighbours.

The O'Hares. Irish trash!

His father, staggering by then with the drink taking its full effect, fumbling the belt from his work trousers and the buckle ripping into Bob's soft white buttocks, his little hands trying to fend off the blows. The chill of fear. The loathing and the art he had almost mastered of separating himself from the scene by becoming mesmerised by the chink of light from the street lamp outside the fence, gleaming through the corner of the shed where the roof met the wall.

The disappearing trick of it.

He remembered the mocking, slurred accusation.

'Just like your mother! Weak! You're weak! Weak!'

A blow for every word. He had steeled himself even as a little fella. And he made his vows as his childhood was left behind. 'No one. Ever. Will do this again. I'll show them. No one. Ever.'

After the beatings in the shed Bob would creep back to bed. Slipping past his father still staggering in the garden beds, now exhausted from effort and spent emotion, from a week on the roads driving the heavy machines for the Council, from the rum, from his own treachery, his own pain, just the pain of living. Don O'Hare was never the same since the war. Like so many of them.

His best mate blown up in front of his eyes. Saw action in the jungle. Saw too much action. That was when the fear came into his mother's eyes. Unspeakable nightmares, his father calling out, looking for his army gun, yelling in the night.

And his mother shushing his father, calming him, "there, there," rocking him in her arms like a baby. Hearing his father's quiet urgent sobs racking his body, shaking the bed, harder to hear than the yelling.

Always his mum, whispering to him and his sisters, 'Quiet now. Don't upset your father. You'll be for it.'

Bob had grown up knowing that his father was lost to him forever, pulling up the blankets around his head, looking for comfort in the night, a great tangle of legs and small bodies struggling down to the oblivion of sleep.

His mother standing just inside the door stony-faced, arms outstretched, unable to speak but unable to rescue. Arms of salve and assurance but not of safety. Not yet. He would lie awake in his wet bed waiting for the morning. Wanting the light in the corner of the shed to reappear in his own bedroom so he could disappear into it forever and never come back.

Sometimes his father would spend his nights on the loose in the house, like a wild escapee from the zoo. He remembered the sounds coming from his parents' bedroom, softer now but just as urgent through the paper-thin walls then ... nothing. Only the whimpering of his mother for a little while before the world closed down for the night. His world. The world of little Robert Patrick O'Hare, lying in his wet bed unable to move for fear. He tried to drive away the little niggly fringe thoughts of hate and contempt for his mother who did nothing to avenge, nothing to protect, nothing to mollify.

His vows began to formulate. 'This is what they're like … women.' Loving the softness of welcome arms, longing for love, for comfort, hating the weakness and passivity that did nothing. Planning to be strong to never show his true feelings, to quickly get the upper hand no matter what. Be in charge. Be the man.

There was one Saturday morning that Bob would remember forever though.

A silent morning, too early for the neighbourhood mowers to begin their Saturday whirring. Bob had heard his father yelling through the night. 'Shut that bloody dog up for God's sake.' Bob had run out into the garden to let Scrag off the leash. The dog had fawned on the ground, licking his bare feet. Next morning, Bob had gone looking for the dog. There in the side garden he found his father sprawled, his mother's blood-red rose bushes clinging drunkenly to his shoulders as if they had imprisoned him. Nearby his father's false teeth lay in a pile of vomit near his mouth. Flies buzzed, busy in the feast. His father just lying there. His eyes were open and staring at nothing and everything. His face a bluish grey. He was dead. The police came. The neighbours came. His grandma came.

'Choked on his own vomit,' they said, shaking their heads ominously. 'Yeah. The boy found him apparently. Poor little bugger.'

He heard the man from over the back fence who was standing in his pyjamas in their yard. 'Good riddance, I reckon. Gave his family a helluva time.'

Then hawked and spat near his father's body where he lay in the garden still. Ants crawling all over his father's face, nibbling.

And his mother standing wrung out like a garment, tiny blackcurrant eyes in her white pudding face looking at the blank wall in the kitchen.

An end and a beginning.

Bob as a teenager had left Tenterfield as soon as he could, leaving his mother and sisters behind in the backwash of his childhood. He'd managed to find work in the demolition yard at Bunjip Bay. Found solace in the rough camaraderie of the blokes at the yard. He found he loved the solitude of fishing on the beach at night. The silence was a sedative. Was good at surf fishing, as it turned out.

He was just inside his twenties when one of the blokes at the yard, Geoff Hefflin, came in one day all excited about a blind date he had set up for them both. A first-ever date for Bob. The first moment he laid eyes on Jenny, with her long blonde ponytail and wide-mouthed smile crinkling up very blue eyes, he'd felt feelings he had never had before. He was swept away by a different tide that threatened to dislodge his footing and dump him in a deep rip going out to sea. Didn't even mind the strawberry-coloured birthmark across her forehead shaped like a map of a small continent. He suddenly no longer felt so alien, left to drift out to sea in a boat with no oars. His tide was coming in. This girl entranced him. Made him feel like a proper bloke. Even a decent bloke. She seemed able to bring him out of hiding. Helped him talk. She was smart too. A tough no-nonsense girl. Knew what she wanted. He felt overwhelmed with the edge of what looked like happiness.

The shadow of unworthiness was never far from him, though.

They'd been dating now for five months. Bob's quietness had fooled her when she first started going out with him. Caroline was

Jenny's forever friend. They'd known each other since Kindy. Gone through school together, then on to Longmore Uni where they both studied Psychology.

Caroline's mum, Celia, was her sort of go-to mother person when in doubt. Both Jenny's family, and Caroline's had been Ten Pound Poms post war. 'The strong silent type, hey?' Caroline's mother, Celia had said, but with raised eyebrows and a smirk. Ha! Silence was not so much golden as filled with unaddressed bleeding wounds, silent rage and locked-in passivity. Silence often crouched like a landmine.

'No comment.' Summed Bob up in two words.

She remembered the look of utter contempt and derision on his face when she suggested how difficult life for his mother had been. The mother rage, buried alive in the very centre of everything was like radium bringing die-off to everything.

It had been a blind date set up by Caroline. There had been days of hope and futures, alight with youthful expectation.

'You'll really like him, Jen. He's really good looking and tall and dark. Just your type. Doesn't say much but I know you can draw him out.'

CHAPTER 2

'Yes. It's a boy, Mrs. O'Hare. Do you want to see him now?'

Jenny's body ached from the long labour but now everything in her physically yearned to have, to hold, to know, to see, to enjoy. This baby boy. Hers. Theirs. At last. Alive. Very alive. Listen to that cry! Elation and exhaustion vied for supremacy. As this little scrap of humanity was laid upon her swollen stomach, reaching with his mouth, sucking at air like a blind puppy, then roaring at the world like there was no tomorrow, she released all her own pent-up emotions joining him in the flood, and with one volcanic pouring cried relieved tears of many emotions.

The nurse who had been with her for the last three hours — the hard hours — brought Bob in from just outside the door. It had become too overwhelming for him before, and he stood at the bedside, awkward with feelings that were escaping now like an exploding box of streamers. Unfamiliar tears streamed down his face as he beheld their baby. His little boy.

'Wow! What a little beauty he is! Wow!'

For just a moment their gaze locked them into each other in a bond beyond words, then Bob looked away quickly.

'You done real good! Real good. Gee, I bet you must be tired!'

Laughing now, relieved it was all over and both fine. "Jeez. I'm even tired just watching what you gone through. Glad I'm not a woman, but.'

Jenny quickly buried the disappointment that Bob had not stayed 'til the end, and it joined all the other emotional wreckage in the empty well of care.

The Casuarina General Hospital was a decent size. It was the next biggest town to Bunjip Bay and had about 200 beds. Their Maternity section was old but the care was good. The Government was talking about closing it down but it hadn't happened yet. The whole area was becoming a retirement catchment area, the young ones were going off to the city and what they really needed was Retirement villages with Hostel Care. The Last Resort.

Jenny's last visit as a patient had been about 18 months before. She was 11 weeks pregnant and the pains and the bleeding had begun mid-afternoon. The whole thing was like a white blur. It had been her third miscarriage and grief had been her constant companion during those early years of her marriage. They said it had been a girl. The nurse said she wasn't supposed to tell her but she did anyway. She wasn't supposed to give her a hug either. Regulations. A kind nurse with a pair of huggy-mummy arms when she needed it. Jenny had partly given up then. That was when Bob really began to drink and drink hard. It was that and the job loss as well. Later on, it had been Caroline who said that sometimes separation came between husband and wife after the loss of a baby. All she felt was empty. Again.

Bob had taken it hard and dealt with it in his own typical way.

'I'm not going through all that again. No way. That's that! You're not going to fall and that's the end of it. I dunno why you want to keep putting yourself through it all the time, it's not right.'

A man's view. Bob's view.

She knew the afternoon that Daniel was conceived. Sex had become a means to an end, a comfort for him and a pregnancy for her. Hopefully. A grudging act on both sides. More a taking than a giving. She and Bob had become even more distant. Jenny had swallowed her grief like a rotten apple that lay festering and rancid somewhere in the unknown. A seedless fruit. Bob had no comfort for her and in his own pain, anaesthetised with more beer, had withdrawn even more.

They had both been tired after a morning at the beach watching waves breaking. They had walked along the beach a bit, Bob talking to the fishermen along the edge of the surf. It was too cold to swim now that May was here. They even had a bit of a laugh together. In a rare occurrence, Bob put his arm around her waist as they walked. Back home, they snuggled up together, warm under the covers, and it was a quiet, slow love-making that had seemed to belong to an earlier era when there was no frenzy or anxiousness about them.

She lay there afterwards with a kind of knowing that a child had been conceived but not daring to move or even think about it. Just knowing, as women sometimes do.

They held their breath. Three months, four, six months and right up to term. And here he was all pink and fuzzy-cheeked and smelling of the cleanest purest scent, all soft down. He was here. In the here and now. Never mind the future or the past. She had a baby boy. Daniel Derek O'Hare. Derek, after Jenny's dad. Nurses came and went with starched efficiency and three days passed. She took him home to fill the waiting cradle. At last.

Danny was a quiet achiever. A seemingly contented child. The only person able to make Bob laugh and forget the troubles at work — when it was available — driving the trucks for the Demo yard. Jenny looked at this source of her joy and wondered what on earth he had to do with Bob.

Daniel, the progeny of those early years. A reason to rise on every troubled morning.

The change in Bob had been slow and imperceptible like a secret tidal surge going at a snail's pace. Jenny loved her Oncology Nursing and the camaraderie of the girls on the Ward. He got laid off the Demo yard and only got called in when they were really busy. Surf fishing became his one escape.

'I said I want coffee and I want it now! Whaddya mean we're out? Are ya stupid? Haven't you got a brain in your head? You don't have to do that much with it, just don't run out of coffee. Struth! Not that much to ask is it?'

Bob never said her name. Not in all the time they'd been together. That would be too much acknowledgement.

'My name is Jennifer. Jenny if you like. Say it. Just say it, What's wrong with you?' she muttered as she left the room.

The cauldron boiling. Steam rising. Bubbles spitting, stinging. Toil and trouble all right. Like the bit of spittle in the stubble on his chin right now. Without moving her head Jenny saw at the edge of her eye

Daniel's blond thatch, as he bent over his painting book on the floor. Hearing but not entering in. He glanced up quickly and caught her eye then looked away. Bending back to his task.

Gazing unblinking at the parked car in the driveway, Jenny could hear the familiar entrapment clunking into place again. Slot. Slot. The steel yoke of obligation and duty heavy on her neck. Her shoulders ached with it. Literally. Cut glass fragments clashed in her head, loud enough to almost hear. The endless sword fight. The pen is mightier than the sword. Her father always used to say that and he was right. He had never said enough to Hermione though. Well, nothing that was enough to keep her at home. Words. Still her one escape. Under cover. Her cover. Bob always watching. Disapproving.

'Y've always got yer head in a book! Fat lot of good that'll do yer!'

Not moving, yet feeling that familiar tight coil in the pit of her stomach. The tiny cold knot of fear. Show nothing. Don't give him the satisfaction. She blinked twice. Be calm, she told herself. Be calm. Her face a mask to the cut and thrust of the words.

At least its only words. At least he doesn't hit me. Well, not much.

A slight smile began as she recalled her friend Caroline saying to her with an exasperated rolling of the eyes. 'Yes, he does. And it's wrong! You just don't see it as that. At least! For heaven's sake! You compare and minimize. Everything's relative.'

Friday afternoon. Air so humid you could just about swim in it. Jenny felt the rivulets of sweat coursing down her back under her top. She scooped up her long blonde hair into a ponytail with an elastic band. No air to breathe. She loosened the folds of the blue sarong tied around her hips. It would be a long hot summer. Already heavy grey clouds gathered low over the horizon, breathing threats. Moody place, Bunjip. A low rumble of thunder rolled around the house as if in agreement, making casual promises of rain.

She reached up to the top of the fridge and grabbed her car keys. Slowly, now. Stay out of range of the arm. Swift as lightning sometimes. Walk across the eggs.

A shadow fell across her as she turned to go. 'Hey. You going or what? Just teasing,' Bob said as he pinned her to the wall, blocking her way. Not a laugh. More a rattle.

'I'm going. I'm going.' She clenched her teeth holding her breath as she ducked under his arm and left the house and its brooding presence.

CHAPTER 3

She slammed the door of her car a little harder than usual and glanced back at the front door where Bob stood, hands on hips, head on one side with a smirk. The old Commodore shuddered into life and moved off down the long driveway bordered by Poincianas and Jacarandas. Full bloom in a profusion of mauve and crimson, the bells of Jacaranda flowers were beginning to carpet the gravel drive. All the signs of a Northern Rivers' summer.

In a few minutes she found herself driving away from Bunjip Bay towards the Estate of Box Ridge Park to Bernadette's house. Safe haven. For now. She rolled the window down and felt the rush of cool air coming off the Bay. She drove alongside the wide stretch of the Bay, its sands sweeping wide and long beside blue and tranquil waters. Round the corner was the Seven Mile, the quiet windswept plains of sand and dunes going on forever. Another land. Away from the sound and blue of the clean ocean of Bunjip Bay, population 5,200. This was her place. The Bay.

All windows down. The steady hum of tyres on bitumen. Nearing the Estate, she passed the Ti Tree lake, whose tea coloured waters were great for swimming, made your hair and skin so soft except Jenny found the lake with its murky depths, threatening. You couldn't see your hand in front of your face. A little boy had drowned there only two summers ago. Hard to find the body with the water that colour. Never did. Now there was a sign put up by the council warning about the deep waters. You could never imagine how deep they were. What secrets they held.

It was Christmas holidays again and a typical January with the silent shimmer of midday heat. The day exhaled hot air with no escape. Children were diving in and out of the lake, cutting the thick humid air with their shrieks. Jenny sighed as the hot steering wheel slipped through her sweating hands. Another heat wave, like last year's and the one before that. This place. Families went to the new shopping centre just to sit for a bit in the air conditioning. Last summer the electrical shops in town had actually run out of fans and cooling appliances.

As Jenny drove further away from the coolness of the ocean she made sure all the windows of the car were wound down so that what little air there was, was able to circulate. Rivulets of sweat ran down the inside of her halter neck, already sticking to her back. Clumps of Ti trees with their salmony-brown peeling paper bark stood like sentries on both sides of the road. The quietness was compounded only by the relentless rise and fall of a chorus of cicadas. The sound of an Australian summer.

Jenny hung her arm out of the driver's side window, driving with the other hand on the wheel. The Ti trees were thinning out now as the first fibro shacks came into view.

The Box Ridge Government Housing Estate. The poverty belt always on the fringes of towns all over Australia. The fringe-dwellers. It had always been a place where they put the Aboriginal families along with the whites on the poverty line. Hard enough to survive on the benefits let alone without a car and far from the minimal public transport. Little boxes made of ticky-tacky like Pete Seeger's old

31

song. And, yes, they did all look just the same. Row after row of grey, unpainted fibro houses, surrounded by the usual mango trees, if you were lucky. Mangoes lying half eaten all over the ground from the fruit bat raids all night long. Fibro, or asbestos sheeting had become the wonder product for builders everywhere. No one knew the dangerous disease lurking in the fibres.

The houses here were mainly unfenced properties, sitting up on stumps a few feet above the ground. Freezing in winter, and stinking hot in summer. Front yards spilling into other front yards with a profusion of kids and dogs and uncollected newspapers rotting at the fence line. A pervading atmosphere of poverty oppressive as a storm cloud, met her full in the face as she rounded the corner to Eden Road. Bernadette and her husband, Trevor lived here with their brood of kids. No Eden here.

As she drove past, she grinned at several barefoot children in various states of incomplete dress. They pulled faces and made obscene signs at her, their faces already filled with the hopelessness and anger. Already ebbing and flowing. A seed bed of squalor and the choking of dreams. All staring unblinking. All waiting for something to happen. It reminded her of a science fiction book she had read as a teenager. The Village of the Damned.

Jenny gave a guilty shudder of gratitude that she didn't live in this ghetto-like enclave. Bernadette's house was an oasis in the middle of nothingness. There was an inescapability in it all. They were prisoners trapped in their own mindsets who preferred the seeming safety of greyness, drabness, no longer seeing the walls as imprisonment but as sanctity, safety from the other-worldness out there.

Jenny put on her bravest face and cheered up in the hope of coffee, comfort and hope for the moment. She peered through the fly screen that was covered in Jesus signs and stickers. A little cultish but a haven nonetheless. Can't complain. Port in a storm really. Signs of life, signs for the unwary, the intrepid and the lost. The door said it all, no conversation required.

Read your bible, it'll scare the hell out of you!

Fair enough.

Bernadette was her religious friend. Bob called her a freak and a cult-woman. But Jenny had known Bernadette before she had become a member of a small but highly excitable local church, which, if you gave it its due, was one of the few groups to actually bother with the streeties and homeless bunkered under the bridge. Bernadette had always had a kind heart and a kind word, and goodness knows Jenny needed both. Bernie seemed to be able to get her back on track with her marriage. Always with a lecture though.

She rattled the door.

'You there, Bernadette?'

Jenny opened the fly screen door, which jangled under its weight of clichés and slogans, and called out again. She wandered down the hallway, stepping over discarded toys and assorted debris on the way into the lounge room that was full of faded country clutter, with a predominance of dried arrangements, swathes, swags, frilled tissue boxes and flowers on everything, and not a single surface left undecorated. Dried flowers, paper flowers, silk flowers, but nothing alive that might run its own gamut of life to wilt and to die.

On a wall was a velour tapestry of the Last Supper and on the coffee table an eagle in black and gold.

Bernadette came flying out of the kitchen wiping her face on a tea towel, thin greasy brown hair hanging in sweaty streaks around her face.

'Sorry, Darl, didn't hear you. Just been doing some cooking for the kids and Trevor. They're just hangin' out for some Lamingtons. I know it's too hot really. She stopped mid-sentence, studying Jenny's face

'Hey, are you OK? Or what?'

Jenny rolled her eyes and sank down into the chocolate-brown corduroy of the modular lounge which disguised a hundred vegemite finger marks, spilled coffee and other assorted grunge. Jenny was grateful for some respite. 'Yeah. Yeah, I guess. Just Bob really.' She sighed long and hard and stared at the ceiling.

Bernadette looked at her with her familiar, I-know-this-will-hurt-but-I'm-saying-it-for-your-own-good expression.

Jenny often ran to this port in her storms when she had reached the end of herself and couldn't quite move on. Bernadette had a way of disentangling the issues from the feelings but also managed to make Jenny feel masses of guilt about the feelings she did have. Well, the honest ones anyway. Jenny had found herself confiding less and less in Bernadette and more in Caroline. Jenny felt her mind wandering off as Bernadette went up a gear for the lecture.

Jenny had almost hidden her deepening friendship with Caroline from Bernadette and definitely from Bob, feeling they wouldn't understand and even possibly disapprove of such assertive and challenging views on life, in fact, on her life. Somehow Caroline's thoughts and attitudes were starting to make sense with crystal clarity.

34

Jenny was already regretting this trip to the Estate, knowing a moralistic edict was about to drop. She moved to the edge of the lounge trying to avoid the worst of the grunge and smears, and half-tuned into what Bernadette was saying.

'Look, Jen, I'm sorry to have to say this and I love you, but you're in this for life. Life is about choices. You've made one.'

Bernadette pushed the damp strips of hair off her forehead. Jenny noted there were black circles under her once pretty brown eyes and a weariness that cloaked her like a second hand cardigan. Bernadette looked pretty tired and miserable these days. Three kids plus Trevor seemed to be taking its toll. Badly. She never bought her clothes from anywhere but the Op shop. Everything was second hand. Trevor didn't like his wife looking too glam. Her life had never really left the 50s, but she always had a cuppa on the go and an encouraging word for most people just when they needed it. Up 'til now, anyway.

She continued on, 'It's 'til death us do part. You know? And that's it. You just need to love him more, and he'll change, you'll see.'

Bernadette's words hung in the air. Jenny always switched off in conversations when people included the fateful, 'I love you but...' She sighed. Everything was getting harder. Best get the coffee and go home. He'd be worse if she was late.

Trevor lumbered his bulk into the lounge room. Overweight and freckly, with his beer belly hanging out of his singlet, ginger hairs sprouting out of his navel like a miniature jungle. He nodded briefly to Jenny, turning his attention to the TV. He wandered over to what had once been a built-in bar, now housing hundreds of cassettes. His hands were grimy with black grease from his job in the local garage. She shuddered and looked away.

People said that Bernadette had religion. Or maybe religion had her. Jenny didn't really understand the pull. Occasionally, she'd accompanied Bernadette to church. They were a lively bunch and the music was non-dirge and fairly up-beat. The people were friendly and not too pushy, but some things sat very wrong with her. Like when Trevor had the affair with the receptionist in the office at the garage when their third child, Ben, was on the way. Everyone knew. Bernadette had pretended not to notice and said nothing. Her pastor turned a blind eye too. Nothing ever talked about, nothing resolved. Jenny had been off on her own tangent again and snapped back to reality as Bernadette was finishing her lecture, tailing off with, '...and anyway. God loves him, Jen."

The phone rang in the hallway. With a groan, Trevor heaved himself up to answer it. Jenny heard him laugh as he leered around the doorframe, looking straight at her with the smug conspiratorial smile she saw on the face of most of Bob's mates. He handed the phone to her. 'It's Bob. For you.' He watched her closely as she answered.

The tightness was returning like a cramp. This time a little dart of acid burned into her throat causing her to wince at the sudden bitter taste. She took the phone and her hand trembled a little. 'Hi, Darl! What's wrong?'

An ooze of volcanic lava blocked all her thought patterns. She placed the phone down on the coffee table and walked away to regain her composure. Then she picked it up as though it was an unexploded bomb.

Chapter 3

'I'll be straight home, Dear. I'm sorry.' She smiled brightly at Bernadette, 'I've got to go home. He's missing me. See you tomorrow. Oh, and thanks for the cuppa. And ... and everything.'

'OK. Come and say goodbye kids. Three small bodies packed into Bernie clinging to her like limpets to a rock. In silence, they waved shyly at Jenny.

She backed the car down the driveway scattering gravel as she went, and drove the homeward road. The breeze picked up as the glint of the ocean came into view. She went into the corner shop at the edge of town to buy the instant coffee. Nearly home. Her heart was beating fast and her breath came in short spurts. As she pulled into the driveway she could see the edge of a brown envelope poking through the old tin letterbox on the kerb. Grabbing it, she glanced at the back. Great. The letter she had been waiting for. She shoved it into the fold of her skirt and ran in.

The brown velvet curtains were drawn in the lounge room where Bob was engrossed in the Sports Show, flicking through with the remote control dispassionately. He held up his hand like a traffic cop motioning her not to talk. She waited quietly by his side for a few minutes not wanting to push the edges, then left the room having dutifully reported in. Let this particular sleeping dog lie.

Out in the coolness of the garden all the flowers were bedding down for the night. A spirited family of noisy Miners flew up from the Banksias, cheeping off to another party.

She opened the brown envelope. Her eyes raced to the end of the page.

"Thank you, Mrs. O'Hare, for your application to study Advanced Counselling. We are pleased to offer you a three-year scholarship in view of your Entrance Examination results and your current nursing experience." She smiled the secret smile of possibility and breathed out a sigh of hope. The letter was already back in her sarong.

The punishing glare of the sky during the afternoon had been a great eye that never seemed to close. Shadows began to slant across the garden. An arc of white Corellas flew across the blue, their plaintive cries signalling the end of the day. She longed for the cool green of another place. Anywhere but here with its intrusiveness.

The humidity was almost tangible now. A mist leaving her feeling depleted and without oxygen. Inside Bob was yelling something unintelligible. Jenny closed herself and waited. It rattled her that Bernadette reminded her she had vowed to love him forever. Forever was a very long time. A wave of revulsion swept over her. She thought of Danny. Her son of consolation. I need to see Caroline again, she whispered to herself.

A new secret was coming into fruition. Well, one of them, anyway. She would study, and study hard. Bob must never know. Her insurance for whatever lay ahead. A plan for a future. If there was one.

CHAPTER 4

"Tread softly where I lie inside the prison of my mind. The door is shut, the train has gone. I'm leaving you behind ... you behind..." she carefully penned the lines in her journal then snapped it shut for the day.

Gideon Vale was a great sprawling town inland from the coast in NSW gaining weight and momentum year by year, it had let its belt out and spread throughout the valley. Like every country town, it had the quiet and seemly façade of rural living held up like a set in a Hollywood movie. A favourable glow spread over Gideon Vale in a soft light that appeared to be innocuous, and was never deeply scrutinized. It gathered people to itself, 'til its population reached numbers of a city with settlements flowing up the lower mountain ranges. From the day her mother left the family, Jenny often felt the grey nothingness of invisibility which came on her in shops and waiting rooms. It came too when she allowed herself to begin to actually think instead of act. Or over-react really.

Around about then, she truly believed she was invisible.

It seemed the whole family and the whole world continued about their business, looking straight through her like an unframed pane of glass.

Her arm looked as if it belonged to someone else. There was a sort of standing outside herself and looking in like a separate person. A cutting away from what was happening. Her escape hatch..

Once, she'd started cutting off the tops of the plants in her mother's garden, particularly the fragrant ones like lavender and rosemary, and chopped them up with a garden knife putting them in an old teapot and casting spells all around the house in an effort to make the family invisible too.

Home had been Gideon Vale on the North Coast. The only Pommies in the street. They'd never fitted in. The house was an old Queenslander, high set, peeling cream paint with a green trim. An old fashioned 50s garden with gerberas, hydrangeas and poppies in neat beds beside the path and along the fence line. A big Frangipani leaned over the front gate, and Honeysuckle weighed down the side fence all the way to the back yard. The old metal front gate swung open every dawn morning on rusty hinges yielding right of way to the milkman with his big metal pan of raw milk. She loved Saturdays. No school, safe warm days, the whirr of lawnmowers in peoples' yards, the Saturday aroma of newly cut grass.

She and Fiona tore around with all the crazy kids in the street, skittering about on scooters and in billy carts, building cubby houses up in the pine trees on the spare block down the street. They ran off into the hills, making forbidden fires with stolen matches to cook potatoes in the hot ashes. Jenny stood out from the rest, her long colt legs and golden pony tail easy to spot in the bunch.

Derek Slade, her dad, and husband of the over-precious Hermione, drove a green Morris Minor. Small, conservative and effective, and a slow starter. Like himself. He'd started to teach

Hermione to drive but she had lost interest early, and preferred someone else to drive her to her various destinations. Derek was not the least surprised. She'd never stuck to anything. He had already begun to regret immigrating to such a land of contrasts and contradictions. Not at all what they'd been told back in the old country.

In the long, hot summer nights in Gideon Vale, Jenny would sometimes climb past her sleeping sister and out of her bedroom window, and shimmy down the peach tree to the grass. In the moonlight that often flooded the garden, she was unafraid of the ghostly shadows of the arms of trees. The chickens in their coop would be silently sleeping in feathery heaps waiting for the dawn, signalled by the rust-coloured rooster; the herald of the day.

In the evenings, Hermione and Derek Slade, would sit in the lounge room, well away with their Sherry, listening to the strains of Beethoven on the record player. Jenny, seizing the summer air, knew they would not even suspect that she was not in her safe little bed alongside Fiona.

No television for this family. Now as an adult she was supremely grateful for such a restriction which had hurled her headlong into books. In the Gideon Vale Public Library she'd disappeared into Enid Blyton's caves with the Famous Five and the Secret Seven's mysteries like the newly found friends that they were, running and scampering on the cliffs of England where her heart was sown.

And Hermione — pretentiously named by her mother after a Greek goddess, she was told — never stopped complaining about Australia. She summed up the country in one sentence, 'These people simply have no culture, Dear.'

Her mother had deeply regretted the long ship's voyage, which had spanned over six weeks of rolling grey ocean. Only to find herself bored with the social circle of the town, or rather, the lack of it. Her creativity stifled and starved of the culture of a fortunate London upbringing. Clicking her tongue she'd throw back her head with a derisive, 'Really! These people! This country!'

So Hermione had been deeply dissatisfied with life in general and Derek in particular. Occasionally, Hermione would attend a school meeting and Jenny would catch her mother's withering superior glances at the other mothers as they waffled on and on about the local Parents and Citizens meetings. Hermione regarded these as well beneath her, so rarely attended. There, but not there.

A superior and aloof woman with no friends to speak of. Well, not kindly, anyway.

Jenny's father, a small, quiet people-pleaser, grey in colour, nature and in outlook, tried to explain away his wife's displeasure, covering up, embarrassed when she had become too loud, too drunk, too English and too much, even for him.

Hermione sated her emptiness in Sherry and men. Barely clandestine affairs with the occasional travelling salesman broke the boredom and fed her hungers. The Slade family became the talk of the town. Fiona seemed to glide through it all untouched, while Jenny always felt kind of responsible, ashamed at her mother's blatant behaviour about town. It devastated them as a family. When Hermione and Derek were off with the Sherry and the music, Jenny alienated herself as the invisible wall of glass went up between them all. Derek was not a serious drinker but drank to keep up with his wife. The silence between them became a moat around each individual castle.

Then there were her mother's frequent trips to hospital following blood-soaked mornings, when all the bed linen had to be placed in the big concrete tubs in the laundry, followed by the now inevitable door-slamming rows that erupted between her parents into the late hours of the night, often following her mother's discharge from hospital.

Derek was a tired man. He was tired of their life, tired of living and tired of his wife's affairs underlining her cold rejection of him.

They became dreamy days for Jenny. She viewed life through her own fantasy window, when she cared to open it. Like so many children, she imagined she was adopted, a princess from a faraway land, a changeling, biding her time with these earthlings, waiting for her real parents to come and collect her.

Until that summer. The summer their lives changed into something unrecognisable.

The lazy haze of cicada-buzzed heat domed over the town. The surrounding hills were blue with eucalypts, unmoving as the heat mantled itself about them with its promised lethargy.

The girls had not seen much of their mother in those last few months. Derek didn't discuss his wife's long absences from home. This time it seemed he'd given up. As though a light had gone out on the inside. For good. He fell into the habit of leaving the back porch light on and the key in the door. Just in case. The girls never asked.

One night, Jenny heard a muffled noise from his bedroom. Was he crying? The loud rows had come to an end replaced by a world of nothing. A vacuum of unanswered questions.

Late one night she had tiptoed out into the hallway and heard her Mum talking in a pleading voice.

Mummy!

Jenny ran toward the kitchen, but just as she reached the closed door, she heard the crash of something heavy hitting the floor. Then shattering glass. Her mother was crying loudly. Derek's voice rose about her sobs. 'Just get on with it. I don't care anymore. It doesn't matter anymore. It's over anyway.'

A door slammed. Jenny tiptoed back to bed and lay quiet and still for a very long time.

And, it was over. A sadness like an unexpected death settled on the Slade family. Derek rattled around inside the house, a grey spectral presence in a mausoleum.

Without Hermione, the house was an empty shell. A heavy fog submerged them all, making it hard to see and hard to move.

CHAPTER 5

Mrs. Olivia Hallows lived next door to the Slade's in a Grimms Fairy Tale kind of house. Her little front path was bordered by Pansies and Sweet Williams. An arch of tiny pink roses surrounded the doorway. She'd lived there alone for as long as Jenny could remember. Her husband had never returned from the war. Missing in Action they said. MIA. Both neighbours generally kept to their own side of the high wooden-paling fence.

Before Hermione left home for good, Olivia would come in and have a cup of tea with her. Not quite friends, they had enough in common to keep a thread of conversation from breaking in the middle, becoming unravelled.

Hermione talked of her as Mrs. H, as though she were elderly, but really they were around the same age give or take a couple of years. 'This war changed us all, Dear, didn't it? My Fred just never came back. Don't know if he's dead or alive.'

Hermione regarded her as far too uninteresting to bother with. It had been after one of Hermione's discharges from the hospital that Mrs. H had invited her over. Her only comment to Derek, when she returned was, 'She doesn't even read, Dear! No bookshelves. Nothing.'

Jenny liked her well enough and she was company sometimes on the weekends or after school, when Dad was busy and she was bored with Fiona and all the street kids. She let Jenny cook sometimes and cut out pastry with animal shapes. Let her use the tiny edible silver balls and hundreds and thousands to decorate the tops of biscuits. She was old, to Jenny.

One night, Jenny was out of bed wandering in the garden under a full moon which was hanging like a great balloon in an inky sky. She was careful to be quiet so as not to disturb the chooks. She was humming to reassure herself in the dark, when suddenly she saw the figure of a man climbing Olivia Hallows' fence. The odd thing was he had his hat on, a daytime going-out hat, along with a suit and tie. He clumsily flung his leg over the wooden-paling fence. She heard the tearing of cloth, as his trousers snagged on something and she heard low swearing like a growl. The man dropped down to the garden below, landing like a cat, looking around him warily.

Jenny remained rooted to the spot, holding her breath, sure he could see her. They were only feet away from each other, but if she did her invisible trick, it should work. The man moved into the darkness but as he passed under the glow of the street light shining into the garden she recognised him. It was old Mr. Cooper from three doors down. How strange! What was Mr. Cooper doing in the middle of the night jumping over fences?

Jenny crept up to the fence where she knew there was a paling missing, her heart thumping. She peered into Mrs. Hallows' garden. At the illuminated back door she was shocked to see Mrs. Hallows, almost unrecognisable, under the light of her back porch.

There she stood, in what looked like a filmy, gossamer gown blowing about her as light as air, the outline of her body visible underneath. Her face was made up as if she was going on the stage to perform. In high heels, her legs teetered on the edge of the step.

Bending her body in half she leaned forward with her eyes closed and her lips pursed ready for a kiss. In her hand she held a full glass. With a rush, Mr. Cooper launched himself at her, the glass fell into the darkness splintering somewhere below the stairs and with a little shriek Mrs. Hallows was swept inside, the door slamming behind them both.

Jenny avoided her after that as she was uncomfortable around her but not quite sure why. She learned to cook in her own kitchen from then on. She had her best friend, Caroline, just a few doors down to play with now. Caroline didn't laugh at her funny ways or ask any questions about what had happened to her mother. They rode their bikes to the local pool and hid away from Fiona under the back yard trees, reading their books.

After her tenth birthday and the day of the ballet that never happened, everything had changed. Once again, fodder for gossips. The family whose mother left Derek to bring up the girls on his own. Gone off with the bloke that sold women's clothes door-to-door.

Derek Slade seemed to diminish and recede into nothingness. Even his job with Evan and Evan Accountants seemed to disappear. It was as though he vaporised and disappeared along with Hermione. Resentment trickled in like treacle in milk, colouring the family.

Jenny studied hard, excelling dutifully, proving a point. On her fourteenth birthday, she hoped against hope for a visit from her mum. Nothing. Not even a card.

'You're a big girl now,' her father had said, 'We don't need to have a party. It'll just be us.'

Not really a birthday at all. Derek did his best rallying the girls. Fiona was twelve. Between them all they ran the house in slap-dash chaos. Jenny carried a heart full of hope for a future she could only dream about. It rarely had anything to do with her dad or Fiona. Or her mum. Or even Gideon Vale. That was before Bob.

CHAPTER 6

A new secret was hatching itself into Jenny's reality. Well, one of them anyway. She would study and study hard. Bob must never know. Her insurance for whatever lay ahead. A be-prepared decision for the future. If there was one.

Jenny walked in to the coffee lounge, eyes darting everywhere, trying to spot Caroline. She and Geoff had been separated for quite a while now. Caroline seemed relaxed. Happy, even. She looked like the weight of a thousand years had lifted off and flown away.

The Oasis was off the main beach-front where a quieter clientele managed to meet. It was where the local and visiting surfies didn't go. Most people tended to congregate on the front where the cheaper burgers-and-shakes joints were. It had piped music and art for sale on the walls. Mainly colourful abstracts. The same paintings had been on the walls for at least the last couple of years, but it seemed to add a touch of class in a beachside town like Bunjip Bay.

It was late afternoon and the ocean breeze had picked up nicely. The local fishermen and holiday makers were making their way down to the beach now in the cool of the day, walking in the shadow of the headland as the sun relented its grip and began the slow slide down.

The little path winding down to the beach was full of exasperated mothers waiting for the long summer holidays to end so that normal life could resume with school going back. Bunjip Bay swelled in numbers considerably in the summer holidays. Surfers from all over coming down for the big ones, and families occupying the little beach cabins all around the Bay area. By the end of January, Bunjip was tired of the tourist invasion and wanted their town back.

It was still a few hours to go before Jenny started her evening shift at the hospital. Glad she'd done her four years training at the City Hospital. It had been a huge slog and hard study years but she had done well. Considering.

She found Caroline draped gracefully over a lounge at the back of the shop. Caroline had begun to talk to her with words that sounded, well, out of her realm of reference. Words like "co-dependency" and "responses to reactions." All that psychology and stuff. But it made sense, a lot of it. Particularly the stuff about "separating away emotionally" and "choosing your response instead of reacting to his reaction". Blah, blah, blah. As Jenny listened she could feel her walls beginning to crumble, the fortress falling. The belief system she hid behind. Was this the "feminism" the papers were talking about? Were women really burning their bras? What self-image? Did she have one? Who the heck am I? Does it even matter? Dunno. As far as she and Bob were concerned, didn't they say "opposites attract?" What he doesn't have, I do. But now I think about it, there's not a whole lot in him that I would really even want to be a part of. Caroline whooshed down the last of her cappuccino.

Jenny scraped a chair out to sit down.

'Where you been? I was ready to give up on you.'

'Oh, just that Bob...'

Caroline held up her hand and looked away. 'Oh, look, don't tell me. Same old, same old.'

Her mouth was a straight line under a sentence too difficult to say.

'I've got some pretty exciting news, Caroline.' Changing the subject, Jenny sneaked the brown envelope out of her handbag like an illicit drug.

'Look at this.'

Caroline opened it up and skimmed over the contents. Her eyebrows shot up and she smiled wide.

'Well then. That is fabulous. You going to take it up? What about your dear husband?'

Ignoring the jibe, Jenny tapped her fingers on the table between them nervously.

'I want to do this. I really do. Not sure whether to tell Bob or not.'

'Well,' said Caroline, signalling the waitress to the table. 'You'd be mad to tell the bugger. He will only talk you out of it. I know how these things go with you and him.'

Jenny ordered her coffee, frowning. 'Look. I love the Oncology Ward. The work, the patients. I do. But ... I just want to finish what I started once. Somehow, this is going to happen.'

Caroline was full of plans, good news and her single-parent life. 'Craig and Corey are absolutely fine. They go to Geoff at weekends. He's still pretty angry but...' she shrugged. Caroline checked her watch and stood up, scooping up her cane bag.

She turned to Jenny. 'You have been listening to what I think, haven't you? I'd hate to see you waste the rest of your life on that loser.'

Caroline swished away before Jenny could answer. She slumped back in her seat, trying to process it all.

CHAPTER 7

Jenny used to love psychology once. It was her Major at that first exciting year of University before she met Bob. Got in on a scholarship there, too. Top of her year at school back in the sixties. Bob didn't like her getting an education. Said he felt it was unnecessary particularly as she was going to be his wife one day. After all, he had left halfway through high school and what harm had it done him? So she gave it up. After only one year. Did it for him. Until now. Of course the nursing course was different. More fitting for a girl than being a psychologist. What was she thinking? Reading enough books as it is. Now the Counselling Course had come along just at the right time. Posted on the notice board in the ward room at the hospital. It fairly leapt out at her. And now she was in. The text books would be sent to the hospital address. The old typewriter that had been her dad's still worked. Hopefully.

She flashed back to the childhood years, lolling about in the town library ravenous for book after book. The great escape. Words ingested and now part of her fabric

Five years as a Latin student had taught her to understand derivations. The challenge of translating Ovid and other Latin literature and the great joy of conjugating verbs and breaking them up into parts. Unusual maybe, but almost mathematical as well. The other kids in the class thought she was crazy liking Latin of all things. No use to anyone now.

Remembered the great pile of library books carefully stashed like treasure in her bike basket, riding home fast to indulge in like secret chocolate. She had given it all up a few years after she married Bob, devoting her time and energy into meeting his needs and those of the household. Like an alcoholic laying aside the booze. But every now and then the longing would return to remind her of who she was.

She had had a dream recently. She woke in a sweat, sat bolt upright in bed, frightened.

It was about an emaciated, prematurely aged woman looking hideously grieved crawling across the floor of a dark cavernous dungeon strewn with cobwebs and dust barely making it to the door, and thundering on the heavy, metal-padlocked door to be let out or she would die. Bit of an intense one that. Something in the hunger and desperation reminded her of someone. She dared not look at the face. A soul rising unannounced. Back from the dead and not laid to rest. Right there.

There was always the dilemma of untouched desire. Easier to leave it under the bed with the rest of the hidden agendas, broken promises and dreams cut in half by catastrophe and life.

With Caroline's words ringing in her head, she walked through the house she had worked so hard to furnish and pay off. Bob didn't like working for a boss anymore, didn't like someone else calling the tune. They had fallen on hard times in the last few years. He'd been laid off at the Demo Yard and nothing much else had come up. Certainly nothing in Bunjip along those lines. They had drifted into the pattern of it all now. Thank God she had her nursing to fall back on. Jenny was mainly happy to bring home the money every week for Bob to decide what to do with.

She sat out in the garden on the lazy-boy lounge under the Lilli-Pilli tree until the sky darkened, and coolness began to drift in borne on a sea breeze. Families of blue wrens pipped in the tight bushes on the back fence, settling for the night. She could hear the muted hum of a cheering crowd on the telly inside.

She had always longed to travel somewhere. Anywhere really. And not just in her mind. She often had a sense of not belonging in this vast hot continent, and thought with nostalgia of a place that was green, misty and vaporous. England would be fine. It was where she had begun her life after all.

Both she and Caroline had lived in opposite parts of England when they were small children. That's what had drawn them together as kids. Jenny had come from Cornwall in the south, the cries of the gulls a permanent echoed memory now, and Caroline had been brought up in the North West of England, in an old mill town that had seen better days. They had both migrated as five year olds just after the war with their families who had grown tired of the rationed food and the desperation of the times. They came to Australia, the "land of opportunity" to make a new start for their families. Ten Pound Poms, they called them. She and Caroline had laughed together about being colonials and "ex-pats," and of one day returning to the mother country. A bit of nostalgia really but truth in it too. Probably too good to be true.

She imagined being in London, the London she pictured from books and films. The pigeons in Trafalgar Square, red double-decker buses and the Houses of Parliament. She longed for the excitement of finally "coming home" to her native country. Bob had not understood the pull towards a different shore, a country she barely knew, and his comment was always, 'Huh! Don't see why you'd want to go belting off to a wog country like that! Full of eccentrics! You haven't even seen your own country yet! What's wrong with seeing Australia?'

It was a typical reaction.

It wasn't about what was wrong with Australia. It was about a deep yearning for a life other than this. One with a coolness, a wetness without humidity, a gentle, green span of foliage, of woods and coppices, cliffs and quiet ocean. A water colour instead of a louder-than-life oil painting. Even the words were gentle. More a feeling than something verbalised with any sense of understanding. At least from Bob.

There were times like these that Jenny realised they simply could not connect on any level of understanding about many issues. A walling out. Or in.

Jenny would sometimes stand on the shores of the ocean at the Seven Mile and gaze like Columbus out across the water seeing far beyond the horizon to other shores, other countries, other oceans, other peoples and cultures. She could imagine why they used to think the earth was flat and she imagined the edge at the horizon with great gushing volumes of ocean cascading down over the edge of the world like some giant over-filled global bath. It was an inexpressible urge to search and explore the known world before it was too late. Too late for what? She didn't know. What she did know was if ever the amazing opportunity came to fly off, she would go. Grab it and go.

CHAPTER 8

Jenny was good at her job. An efficient nurse, caring and compassionate, but not gushy. People often said that about her. Just what was needed in a ward where death lurked around every corner. She seemed able to navigate around the huddles of relatives, locked in their own untouchable griefs, grouping in the hallways, outside the patients' rooms. Polite but detached. Perfect for the job. Her other life where she bloomed. Sure, there was stress in it, working on the Oncology Ward, but she had been there over ten years now and was used to the levels.

There was sometimes the hope, sometimes the recovery, but more often a transition through to the Hospice on the other side of the grounds, where the wind sang its mournful dirge through the Casuarinas. The Last Resort, as they affectionately called it. Sometimes it was hard to detach.

Always her escape from Bob, and a place where she was respected and affirmed by her colleagues as she did her shifts, organising rosters and staffing, trying to fit in with everybody's lives, often at the expense of her own.

There were occasional movies or lunch with a few of the girls, but only if it fitted in with Bob. Every month they bought a lottery ticket, wishing and hoping in a half-hearted way.

It was a late Friday evening and she had left Bob and Danny in their own worlds in front of the TV. Danny jumped up and hugged her as she left, holding on for a bit longer than usual. The wind ripped through the Jacaranda branches as she drove away, dropping a purple blanket across the windscreen. She flipped the wipers on in irritation.

When she came on to do her shift, there were four other nurses, all waiting to go off duty. There was a buzz at the desk and a lot of whispers and giggling. They all looked excitedly at each other and beckoned her into the Treatment Room and shut the door. Jill, usually very quiet and shy, threw her arms around Jenny and shouted in her ear along with the others. 'We won! We won! We won something on the lottery!'

'What? How much? when?'

'You'll never guess. It's second prize!' Everyone squealed.

Her heart was stone. All Jenny could think of was how she would tell Bob.

She kept her secret to herself for as long as possible. As the days and nights went on, and the news broke on the ward, a new resolve began to form in her. She swung from one extreme to the other. From "this was my money and there was no way Bob was getting his hands on it" to "I must tell him. I must give it over to him. After all he is my husband".

Keeping the secret felt like permanent indigestion. She thought long and hard about it as she walked the Seven Mile alone in the early mornings, frightened to tell, frightened not to. The longer she waited the more furious he'd be.

There was more than enough to book a return fare to England and have a decent three week holiday.

The silence spread between them daily, an ever-widening gap into gulf country. You in your small corner. And I in mine. Not a glimmer of light to be had.

One evening when Bob had not gone to the pub, she resolved to tell him. The baked lamb was flavoured with guilt as she determined that this was the night to tell. With her heart hammering, she began her launch of news.

'Bob, I've got something to tell you.'

His hand clenched tighter around the can of beer. Not even a grunt.

She was left in the space.

He didn't look up from the TV. With a snort he lurched up like a great bear and walked out of the room. Out of the house and into the car. The door slammed like a final word. Jenny was rooted to the spot and she realised she was holding her breath. The exhale was like the hiss of a puncture. She turned to go into the kitchen for some tea. The front door opened again. Her cup crashed to the tiles, smashing in half. She waited. Nothing.

She heard the metallic click as Bob heaved back in the old recliner. He lazily flicked to another channel, moving like a dog into a basket.

'Ha!' He gave a laugh like a choking creature waiting to die.

The three of them ate the baked dinner in stony, cutting silence, with only the clatter of cutlery on china to break it.

Danny slid off his chair like a cat, and was away to his room as soon as he could. Bob continued shovelling baked potatoes and gravy.

'Help your mother with the dishes.'

Danny turned back, his face closed and wary. Jenny crept down the hallway and into bed. She lay awake a long time, watching the pattern of the moon shining through the curtains.

The next night the footy was over on the telly. He stretched back in the recliner with a beery belch, spilling newspapers off his lap and onto the carpet.

Jenny sat on the edge of the lounge, biting her nails to the quick. She tried again

'Bob. I've got some good news.'

`He flicked the channel. Sound ripped into the air.

'That right ? Out with it then. Cat got your tongue?'

She took a deep breath. 'Its ... it's a lottery win. Some of us have won some money.'

He pretended not to hear. Flick. Flick.

'Ha! Wondered when you'd let us in on the secret. Yeah. Kev told me last week down the pub. Money hey? God knows we could do with some. And of course, what's mine is yours and vice versa?' Laughed like a strangled chook..

He lurched out of the chair and stood in front of her. Jenny jumped back by instinct. The freeze of fear laid its steely teeth down her spine and robbed the air.

'Boo!' he pretended to grab for her and pawed the air near her face. Laughing, he turned and went clumping down the hall towards the bedroom.

Jenny ran from the house, grabbing her keys as she fled to the car.

The sword fight began in her head. The familiar clash of steel. Cutting, ripping, piercing. And now the to-and-fro of examining her own heart, searching for the way through the maze.

All too hard. I'll just cancel and give it all to Bob.

She tossed and turned most of the night, rolling thoughts around her mind like so many marbles in a jar. At dawn, decision came.

Tuesday morning was a bright, clear-sky day. She rang Caroline.

'You've got to meet me at Oasis! Something fantastic has happened!'

Caroline walked in to the café, eyebrows quizzical, and sat on the edge of the cane seat.

'So? What's your great news? You are finally leaving the moron?'

Jenny buried the prickle quickly .

'Don't be stupid! Better than that!' She placed her hand dramatically over her heart, spacing her news. She widened her eyes. 'You'll never guess! I have won the lottery, Dear!'

They squealed together and hugged each other madly, just like when they were kids growing up.

'And what's more, you and I are going back to England for a trip!'

More squeals. More hugs. People were staring. So what!

She told Caroline about Bob's antagonism .

'Oh, what did you expect? Applause? A trumpet fanfare? Be real, Jen. I'll bet he suggested you give it to him. He'd be absolutely spewing you'd won! And keeping it! Good on you girl! You go for it!'

With Caroline's encouragement ringing in her ears, for the very first time, Jenny stood her ground unabashed against the railings and harassment of her husband. He threatened. He cajoled.

But somewhere deep inside her there was a slight turning in another direction. A compass marking.

Bernadette was a different story. Jenny dropped in one morning, knowing Trevor and the kids were not home. Her stone statue expression said it all, and Jenny knew she already had been told about the big lottery win. She looked at Jenny with cold envy and pursed disapproving lips.

Jenny felt a wall go up between them like a robber with a bank teller.

Bernie's first response, 'But what does Bob reckon? That's very important you know, Jen. And anyway what about that orphanage in Africa I've told you about that I send money to? Maybe they could do with the money more than you.'

Jenny was realising that both Bob and Bernie were as manipulative as each other but in different ways. Then she felt outrageously torn. Forget them all. Simple that way. But then again...

Jenny watched Bernie put her head on one side pursing her lips like a cat's behind. There was never any joy in Bernie's face.

She went home defeated and confused. She so wanted to please everybody. It didn't matter about herself but she so wanted to do the right thing. She wished she'd never bought the ticket and then things could just go along the same. She hated change and the rocking of the boat. She hated that she had done something that looked good, but now everyone seemed so upset by it. Damn it all!

She went to bed early that night and prayed for a sign.

The moon filled the bedroom with inescapable light. A long night ahead. Cicadas raved.

She rolled over trying to drop down into sleep that evaded her like shadow landings.

She booked the tickets as soon as she could get to the Agency and before she changed her mind.

Bob's car broke down. Jenny spent the money to fix it. Bob wanted to do a course in Electronics. She paid for it. He scowled and growled about the place and drank more beer. He began to bring it in cartons, the brown long necks. He brought home take away pizzas just for himself, and began to get fat. The lounge, the telly and the beer became his life. The Electronics course came and went, without Bob in attendance. He no longer conversed with Danny, once his golden-haired boy. There were nights when he went fishing with a skinful of beer, and was gone all night. Nothing satisfied him. Like an animal, there were unexpected wakings in the sleep of the night. A man bent on self-gratification. Jenny felt used and violated.

CHAPTER 9

Jenny juggled shifts at work with her holiday to England. It all came together. They flew from Sydney. Just Jenny and sweet Caroline. She'd been waiting for this adventure almost unknowingly for years. Like two teenagers they escaped, in spite of all Bob's whining.

'What about me and Danny? You never think of anyone but yourself!'

He stood, hands on hips and grim-faced at the front door while she carried her case to the cab. Danny threw his arms around her and buried his face in her neck.

'It's OK, Mum. You go. We'll be fine. I want you to go. You'll be back soon.' He drew back, then whispered in her ear, 'I can always go to Jai's place.'

For the first time in her married life she felt happy. It was a foreign feeling. She tried not to enjoy the first feelings of the joy that came with a Bob-less solitude too much. The guilt of the feeling weighed even heavier, in fact out-weighed the other exhilaration. Balances. Weighed and found wanting. Like blind justice. More like short-sighted justice.

She felt like Pollyanna, promising herself to "think about it tomorrow," as the shelved guilt rushed in to taunt her. Like a professional shelf-packer she astutely packaged it up and put it high on a back shelf for later. England beckoned like a seduction.

It didn't let her down.

England was a year ago now. What a fabulous memory. Black London cabs had whisked them about on crisp spring mornings. Some late snow melted along great, green swathes with daffodils bursting from their long winter hibernation. Cottage gardens and thatched roofs in the Cotswolds had been breath-takingly beautiful. Even the grey wetness of London streets and the crowded Underground had been a memorable experience. One that no one could steal. Hers. Memories began to archive themselves in her mind like so many butterflies shedding colour.

There were no souvenirs to better contain the experience.

The plane touched down at Mascot. Rain sheeted down across the tarmac. Jenny and Caroline searched for the bus to do the final leg of the journey, home to Bunjip.

Jenny was met with a wall of silence from Bob, interspersed with lashings of verbal bullets. Like walking on eggs waiting for one to break. She sensed the gathering storm. The waters closed over again. Danny pounded down the hallway, and met her at the door, grinning hugely, his arms outstretched towards her.

It was an ordinary Friday evening at the end of Summer. "Ordinary," meaning that Bob was down the pub with his mates. The neighbours on one side, Flo and Jim, were out doing the raffles at the local RSL and the rest of the street was probably in bed.

Danny and Jenny were curled up together on the long, yellow vinyl lounge, watching Young Talent Time, singing along. Their favourite.

Bob had been gone for a good while, even before Danny came home from school. This had become a habit more and more on a Friday. Jenny heard the scrape of a car pulling up on the gravel outside. One car door opened. One closed. The car snarled off too fast down the driveway, setting off all the neighbourhood dogs. The back door slammed back on its hinges as Bob lurched into the lounge, swaying in front of them. Jenny gently pushed Danny away from her and he slunk off the lounge like a quiet cat. His bedroom door clicked closed and she heard the key turn in the lock. Jenny felt the knot of steel fear activate in her gut. She sat up on the edge of the lounge, on careful alert.

'Like some dinner?' she said with studied casualness. 'I've kept it in the oven for you.'

With one step towards her, he lunged grabbing her by her pony tail. He marched her across the floor and rammed her face into the wall. His beery breath made her gag and his spittle hit her ear as he shoved her against the pine wood.

'Think yer better'n me doncha? Stupid woman. Just cos yer won all that lovely money. I'll show you.'

She couldn't avoid the hand swooping down. It stung the side of her head, knocked her into the corner of the door. Pain exploded and she slid down the wall. Recovering quickly, adrenalin surging, she backed away from him, skidding across the floor on her back and elbows. He lurched towards her again. She half ran, half crawled out of the back door, running down the gravel path in her bare feet, wincing at the sharpness of gravel on her soles. His drunken tirade bellowed from the door. She reached the end of the long driveway, and began to run along the verge, keeping to the bushes like a fugitive. The car started and revved loudly. The headlights probed the bushes where she crouched.

Danny! What about Danny? Bob had never laid a hand on his boy and she had to trust he wouldn't now. She ran blindly down a small leafy lane that went through the back streets of the sleeping town, then towards the milk bar on the Water front. It was shrouded in darkness. The wind from the sea whipped the awnings into a striped frenzy. Keeping her body crouched still beside a garbage bin, she watched the headlights of Bob's car. It swerved across the intersection and hit the kerb, flattened the No Standing sign, and bounced back onto the road. Bob reversed drunkenly onto the wrong side of the road and drove off.

She left the shelter of the garbage bin and crossed the road to the pavement running alongside the beach. And there before her was the Seven Mile, its calming empty silk stretched out forever under a sullen moon. Taking a deep breath she bent over, her hands on her knees and let the choking sobs overwhelm her, unable to control the shaking. Her head throbbed from the blow. She ran her fingers over her head, making a cautious examination. Stickiness betrayed oozing blood. She stumbled to a sand dune and sat shivering in the cold beach night. The waves pounded the shore. Tide in, tide out.

CHAPTER 10

The wind blew in stronger from the sea, driving itself along the Esplanade, looking for somewhere to land. Tiny spots of rain began to fall like pinpricks on her skin, now goose-bumped. Jenny realised she had only her shorts and a cotton singlet on and began her weary plod off the beach through drifts of sand. Barefoot on the cold pavement, she walked like a robot, through a blur of tears to Caroline's house.

It was after midnight when in a daze, she bashed on Caroline's door. She could see through the shimmer of the front door glass and saw her walking, fastening up her dressing gown, straining forward, trying to see who was knocking at this hour of the night. She opened the door and Jenny fell sobbing into her friend's welcoming arms. After a while, Caroline held her at arms' length, searching her face.

'Good God! Did he do this to you?' The anger rose from some deep place in Caroline and she gently moved Jenny away.

'I'm ringing the police. I don't care what you say.' She was already at the phone on the wall dialling the number. Jenny accepted it all. Drank the sweet tea, washed her face, dabbed at the cut that had now stopped bleeding, and tried to stop crying.

Twenty minutes later a police car pulled up outside Caroline's house and a tall red-headed policeman with a face like a scrubbed potato stood at the door. He took out a notebook and cast a cursory look about the house.

'What seems to be the matter, love?' he said to Caroline.

'Look! See for yourself. My friend has just been beaten up by her husband. I want him arrested.'

The policeman leaned on the doorway, breathing thickly, then casually turned around to the other policeman still in the car with the motor running and the radio blasting.

'Only a domestic, mate,' he drawled. 'Not much here really.'

He put on his professional I-am-concerned-about-you expression and looked down at Jenny, still sitting on the lounge, shaking.

'OK. So just give us your name and I'll make a note of it.' He scribbled in his notebook, then put it away in his pocket. 'Look ... nothing we can do, love. You stay here the night and maybe sort it out with hubbie in the morning. Right?' And he turned and jumped in the car which took off down the street.

The two women looked at each other. 'Sorry, Jen. There's nothing they can really do.' Jenny dropped her head onto her arms.

'I know love, it's not right, is it? That law needs to change somehow. Stay here tonight and I'll come back with you in the morning. You're exhausted. You're not working for a few days. Let's get some ice on that lump on your head.'

It was late the next morning when Jenny and Caroline crept up to the house, afraid of further aggression. The car was rammed into one of the bigger Jacaranda trees, the bonnet and fenders buckled and bent totally out of shape. The front door was wide open. There was no sign of Bob anywhere. Caroline had a tentative look through the house, ready to run if needed. The freezer door had been left open, bait pilchards tipped all over the floor were thawing out in a watery pool of blood. Flies buzzed all over the mess.

They picked up the fish and stashed them back in the freezer and carefully mopped up the floor. Jenny collected some clothes and toiletries and a few other necessities, and they went back to Caroline's. Caroline got Danny from school later in the afternoon. Jenny would leave it a few days before she went home. Call in sick at work. She had loads of sick days to use up.

CHAPTER 11

6 months later

Jenny slid back the door to the back yard and looked around the garden which was drooping after a day of hammering sun. Red and blue Salvias stood to attention and a few red and white Vincas still bloomed. It was dry and there were cracks across the earth where the grass was dying. The Lilli-Pilli was bursting with its cheeky, lolly-pink berries. Sometimes they plopped into her tea as she sat underneath it, leaning back in the cane chair.

Looking in the bathroom mirror that morning, she saw that the cut on her forehead was now a barely visible thin white line.

This year had been long and hot. The garden looked tired and depleted. Even the Hibiscus had folded up its flowers for the day. She would water it all just on sunset, when the cool easterly blew in from the beach. The cicadas were still a full-blown orchestra of deafening sound as the evening sat at the edges of the day awaiting its cue.

She and Bob barely spoke these days; a word truce that suited them both. He had managed to find some work at the Truck Demolition Yard. At least for a season. Jenny did as many evening shifts as she could get, avoiding interaction on any level. Danny had become a self-made prisoner in his bedroom.

Her quiet reverie was interrupted with the sound of the sliding door of the back room, flung back too fast so that it thudded on its runners.

'Where's dinner? Some of us work hard in this family you know!'
He stomped inside, slamming the door behind him.

Jenny leapt up, startled, and ran inside, fumbling for the car keys, ducking under his arm as he straddled the doorway, half blocking her way so that she had to brush past his bulk, odorous and unmoving, the rank smell of yesterday's beer and old sweat that had found its own course down his obesity, filling the air with its pungency.

'Sorry. Sorry. I'll be right back.'

Fear, like an irritating visitor that wouldn't leave, cascaded over her; an icy wash. His faint snigger of victory followed her and if she looked at him, a half-smile of mocking superiority would cover every feature. She kept going.

Afraid to look, afraid to stop or think, she ran to the car grabbing her purse on the way. She revved the motor too hard and turned for the corner store. Maybe spag bol tonight. An easy one and one of Bob's favourites.

CHAPTER 12

It was an overcast February morning. Jenny sat on the top of a sand dune on the Seven Mile with her writing journal, chewing the end of her pen and enjoying the unexpected coolness.

A leaden sea rolled about trying to decide which way to go. A couple of Banded Plovers with neat, black collars strutted about with their little running steps down on the damp sand. A cluster of sea gulls, their feathers ruffling in the breeze, waited patiently to see which way the weather would go.

Only a matter of weeks ago her assignment results for third term had arrived. Two distinctions and one High Distinction. She had smiled to herself as she did a twirl across the kitchen floor.

Bob never suspected a thing and was far too encased in his own Laval cocoon to even notice.

The wind lifted suddenly, sending the dried grass wheels spinning across the white expanse of sand and blowing gritty salt and long strands of hair across her eyes. The Seven Mile stretched forever into the distance, a sheet of moving sand like a mirage as the wind whipped it along. This was her place to be alone. To be herself. The waves began their rhythmic thudding and ominous clouds gathered themselves out on the horizon, a typical cyclone season. The month the kids went back to school, most years. Bunjip Bay was empty now of tourists and surfies. Only the locals kept the place going now 'til the next holidays at Easter.

Australia Day weekend had been and gone.

If a cyclone came though the Bay was renowned for its great swells and massive waves, and surfers from all over Australia congregated to try themselves out in what were very dangerous conditions. Danny was now saving up for a surfboard. A rite of passage here in Bunjip.

The last big cyclone, some years ago, had pushed the beach back, all but removing the gently rolling dunes. It had taken months of council trucks dumping load after load remaking the dunes, recreating its landscape in as natural a shape as possible. Never quite the same again though.

The local council had mounted a project of re-establishing the sand dunes by planting them with sea grass and other vegetation.

It had been the middle of the night in the cyclone season a few years ago when the beach-front houses had been threatened with extinction as the waves lashed their fury and the wind blew with increasing ferocity. Glass had smashed onto the beach and roofs had flown off like great alien birds, tangling up the power lines and plunging Bunjip Bay into darkness and chaos for quite a few days.

She and Bob had come down that night — as did the whole town — to help sand-bag the shore line so that the houses on the front could be saved. It was known as Millionaire's Row, spoken about with characteristic Australian derision, with a touch of mockery and jealousy that some would carry more than others. The old tall-poppy syndrome that was so culturally theirs. The classic Australian put down.

"If they rise up, chop 'em down to your level. Stay in the pit with yer mates!"

But when the chips were down it was all put aside as everyone turned out to help their mates in trouble. It was the Aussie way.

Disaster was a great leveller, right across the board. Even she and Bob worked side by side, together in a different way, working towards a common end. She held the big rough sacks open for Bob to shovel in the sand and others came to lend a hand. Danny was just a little fella, then. Ultimately, the cyclone blew itself out to sea and the houses were saved.

"No Loss of Life," the papers said, sporting a large photographic coverage in The Bunjip Bay Sun, showing the aftermath of unleashed fury across the small town. It was as though a violent, drunken giant had stepped into the town and ripped it up in a night of rage.

Millionaire's Row stood then, perched precariously on the edge of the now non-existent beach, foundations exposed like a skeleton, the sand washed out to sea and threatening to block the sea-way, silting up the channels, but creating a wave form that had brought the surfers from miles around. It's an ill wind...

Humidity had soared. Every house had smelt of mould and damp washing. Fans on in every room but everything still damp. The Estuary had been a surge of swollen brown current, full of branches and flotsam to wash out to sea.

She remembered the trucks of sand coming every day, grinding down the beach, now unrecognisable, eroded down to the bones, gravel and rocks exposed to the thick humid air. Jenny had come down to the beach the day after the cyclone with Daniel and some of her friends with their children. The beach had been covered with thick salty foam like a giant cappuccino. The air was full of the squeals of delight as the children from the town ran laughing through the foam.

Branches had blown down everywhere, and palm trees denuded of fronds left standing like compound fractures where the wind had sent them. Pandanus with their spiky, pale green leaves were uprooted, and some had been totally carried out to sea looking like a Dr. Seuss landscape in the wrong place bobbing around on the waves, trying to decide whether to come in or not. The sea that week had turned a muddy brown with all the deluge of fresh water full of logs and debris from everywhere.

Now it was cyclone season again. Endless rain and unbreathable humidity, salt that crusted on your lips, rust devouring everything metallic with a ravenous appetite. Day after day of heat and wet, the mildew starting on the fibro walls of the houses inside, and the smelly washing hanging limply on lines in the garage, the air too damp to dry anything. Always the rain on the first day back at school in February, but after six weeks of Christmas holidays, who cared?

Jenny gazed out to sea reflecting on her life and the pace it had fallen into. She was always able to write when it was like this. The leaden sky matched her mood. She began to write, the wind whipping the page into a frenzy. Flap. Flap. Flap.

On this February morning
I see waves diamond-studded
Swashbucklers
Glass water horses
Dancing to a final shore.

My one tranquillity in the tearing.
My escape to light.
Take me on the tide that waits
And is not my own doing.
Undo my undoing
Wind me on a spool of light
As silk in the wind.

The rain began to splatter in big, full drops smacking indents on the pages and bulleting into the silvery sand. All too hard. Grabbing everything up she ran to the car park, getting drenched within a second.

Jenny cleared the dishes from their evening meal. Danny, now a reluctant 13, was already ensconced in the quiz show on telly. Bob sat, an impassive mound on the recliner, silent in his own beery reverie, with the day's newspaper slipping off his legs onto the floor. Things seemed to have calmed down at home. For now.

Occasionally at night, when Jenny longed for solitude, time and space away from the dribble and monotony of the polished voices of the television, and the dark thrust and cut of Bob, she would drive down to the deserted sand dunes, ghostly with their silver grass under the moon, with only the ghost crabs scuttling busily from hole to hole, minding their business, scattering softly as she walked amongst them. The ocean called her.

For Jenny, the ocean's real life was in the night hours when waves danced shocked from their somnolent state of the day like a teenager past curfew. Phosphorus dancing. A hussy exhibiting her skirts throughout the night like a can-can dancer, only to disappear down to sleep at the end of the night.

So inoffensive by day but deep and secretive never divulging its oily nocturnal whispers, with only the nonchalance of the moon to observe and spread its gold paving to the edge of the known world.

Dawn came. Grey and leaden as a shark.

It had been a tough few days at the hospital. Two of her patients had died, one in particular to whom she had got close.

Dinner was done And the dishes waiting for Danny to do. Jenny glanced over at Danny and Bob, engrossed in the quiz show. Hated to see the cringy pleasing that Danny gave his Dad, just trying to keep him distracted. Keep him happy. Peace at any cost. Anything to avoid an explosion of rage at his mum. Bob had been fairly subdued after his last violent outburst, particularly after he knew the police had been involved. He had withdrawn like a bear into a cave somewhere deep inside himself, which suited Jenny fine.

'Back soon,' she murmured, exiting the room. They'd never notice.

Throwing a towel around her shoulders, she crept from the house, slid behind the wheel, and eased the clutch out. Scarcely a sound. Free, she drove the ten minutes to the car park at the Seven Mile and stopped in the shadow of a large Casuarina under the only street light in the place. Wind moaned in the trees with their long needles and cones.

Barefoot, she crossed the dunes, still a little damp from the afternoon's downpour, then onto the firm dark sand and down to the water's edge. Walking into the hissing shallows, she felt tiny shells and pebbles glossing over her feet, crusting salt. Her toes dug down into the deeper patches searching for Pippies. The roar, the steady in and out of the waves, comforted her. There was something primal and unchanging with its rhythm sighing in the night.

She imagined sirens singing in the depths calling to one another with their melancholy songs. The call to death. Mermaids lying on the reefs off shore, luring the old wooden vessels to shipwreck, their great bulk drawn by the plaintive cries.

A great starry sky stretched as far as the eye could see.

The ocean was in her night attire: white lace and frothy frills to tart her up.

Jenny lay back in the sand dune amongst the silver, green spinifex. The sand was cold now, soft and silver by moonlight, almost fluid in her hands. A place to be alone and un-accosted. Quiet. No expectations.

She sighed deeply, expelling the day and its dirges. Alone, thinking, all sounds drowned out and the soft night breeze licking at her hair. She adored the solitude of it all, not a soul in sight, after all who would go to the beach at night?

Occasionally the moon outlined a lone fisherman, casting out from the shoreline, bucket at the ready for the catch. The Tailor had been running lately, and in the late afternoon you could watch whole families digging for Pippies with their feet, the tell-tale bubbles on the surface of the wet sand as the waves receded with a soft whoosh. Bob loved the solace of fishing down the beach, coming home with his bloodied haul and heaping them into the kitchen sink to gut and clean later.

Jenny relaxed back onto the cold white sand, stretching her long tanned limbs under a starry sky.

This is magic. She breathed in the thick salt air.

The moon was a great orb of spectral light across the beach. The whole sky was littered with clouds of drunken sculptures the colour of setting plaster of Paris. An exotic frenzy of celestial artists. Medusa heads laughing through the sky in silent dementia.

With the wind pressing, she came alive like no other aliveness anywhere. With anyone.

An oceanic oneness.

She thought of a line from a poem from somewhere way, way away, "I must go down to the sea again, to the lonely sea and the sky."

Yep, that's me, she thought.

Sand was beginning to creep irritatingly into her ears and into the damp patches beneath her eyes. She felt melded with the beach, the crusty salt taste, ancient as days, tingling the tip of her tongue.

Even her hair was the colour of sand and her eyes like the colour of washed denim from too many floods. There beyond the last breakers was a horizon to long for, to wonder what lay beyond it.

The luminous face of her watch showed eleven o'clock. She took one last look at the darkening sky as clouds crossed the moon. The dimmer switch had been activated to change the tone of the night.

No phosphorus on those waves. She walked quickly away from the beach, changing to a sprint now, caught like a naughty child out beyond curfew. Running with resignation, with fear and the dull knowing this was her life. Her heart thudded, anxious about Bob's reaction to her lateness.

She put back the old invisible yoke. With a click and a slam she was in the car, not bothering to brush the sand off her feet. The clutch and brake were harsh and cold on her bare flesh where the rubber had come off the pedals .

She drove the short distance slowly along the road that ran parallel to Bunjip Bay, milking the moment to its last.

CHAPTER 13

A black cat slunk away into the shadows as Jenny inched along her gravel driveway. The lights were still on in the house. The car door opened with a quiet click. The TV blared out into the night.

Probably both still up.

The screen door slammed like a shot. Bob steeped in beer and telly swayed in the doorway. The gulf widening. The Great Divide.

Without a word, Bob stood back from the door and with mock courtesy, he swept his arm across, inviting her in. He staggered off down the hallway towards the bathroom, breathing heavily. You just never knew.

A blonde haystack showed above the lounge chair. Daniel. Still up. Relief flooded her. Bob won't try anything in front of his boy. The buffer zone. She went over to him and put her hands on his shoulders feeling him stiffen as she did it. He was moving away from her these days. Her ally, her unfaltering ally, moving away now. Emotionally, anyway.

The pink cleanness of his scalp reminded her of the dependent years and the gratitude, even awe, at finally having a full-term baby placed in her arms. Quiet even then. Those new-baby eyes looking about the room full of lights and sounds. Like he'd been here before. Hair like straw in the field and just as straight. The survivor of the womb. The quiet achiever people said about him. Really the only achievement that made any sense to Jenny in her own life.

Tread softly, Daniel. Tread softly. Don't take that away from me. Heaven knows there's very little else that's any good.'

Sometimes she would look at him in awe, and wonder what he ever had to do with Bob.

CHAPTER 14

There isn't any black and white
No one dimension thin
The other side is not the same
You'll find if you begin
To open up your mind and let the pieces float about
Kaleidoscopic pictures of a world that's not yet out.

Pulling her thoughts back, Jenny looked at Daniel again, watching him gradually withdrawing from both of them. Her heart and her whole body softened as she remembered his utter blondness, eyes the washed blue of her own, the endless games of hide and seek in the sand dunes down the beach, summers of timelessness that nothing could tilt.

Amazingly conceived in the loving times, the loving days. Calm days, balmy days like sailing in deep waters, gentle days, navigating before the storms broke. The days before Bob's mother, Maureen died and the anger broke loose in him like a beast from the deep. Leviathon, unchained from the underwater lair, bellowing its pain into the hush of their world.

They had gone to Maureen's funeral in Tenterfield. A blasting summer day in mid-January with not a cloud in the sky. The family gathered at the old cemetery, white marble statues standing cold and square like a field of giant teeth. Bob and his three sisters, sullen in black, darting raisin eyes like their mother, each in their own slot. Jenny had left little Danny with Caroline for the day so he wouldn't get in the way. The crows loud and raucous, like so many old black crones on a branch watching from above.

CHAPTER 15

Daniel, the progeny of those early days, became her reason to live and later, to even get out of bed on those walking-on-eggshell mornings. A motivation to be so careful to keep the fragile peace and walk hushed through the mine field of their life. It was like the Emperor's clothes. Everyone knew but him. Jenny in her desperation to have a marriage would say to him, 'We've got to get some help! We need to go for some counselling, or something!'

He would point his thin finger at her, 'It's you who's got the problem! Only crazy people go for help! You go and get help! I'm fine!'

Daniel, predictably bland, the oil on the water, even sometimes the bridge on the waters, peace-making, untroubled, seemingly untouched, but those pale blue eyes drinking, drinking. All-seeing eyes, their wide-angled lens absorbed every scene filtering it through to his heart to write its own story; his round freckled face of trust, fair hair always falling into his eyes with a life of its own. He was a quiet-thinking boy, and, if you didn't know, you could say he was not very bright as Bob's mother had once said about him.

Daniel. The only person in the world Bob seemed to have any heart for. His own son, even though this guileless one had borne the brunt of the sticks and stones hurtling from his father's mouth. Sins of the fathers, and all that.

Jenny felt the ricochet effect on her while Bob needled Daniel about his "insideness," his lack of interest in the footy, in the fishing and all things his father loved.

Daniel, so drawn to the silence of the Estuary at Bunjip Bay, the sound of the wind through the Casuarina trees sighing and singing and keeping him company when he ran from the very different silence of home. At home it always seemed to be full of the echoes of things left unsaid, unfinished sentences too heavy to say.

Everyone said Danny was like his mother. A dreamer. His blond blue-eyed look was Jenny's legacy to him. He and Bob were chalk and cheese on every level. Danny loved sitting gazing at the waves, lying on the sand and imagining in the clouds. Hermione would have loved him. If she'd bothered to stay around, that is.

He loved to simply be alone in the sand dunes, rolling over onto his back, sinking into the silverness of sand feeling its sliding warmth and mobility like silk through his fingers. He had heard that Australia was one of the few places where the sand squeaked as you walked through it. He loved to walk ankle deep in silvery dunes surrounding Bunjip, squeaking his way up and down, pretending snow.

Sometimes he had a recurring dream about a mother. Not quite his own mother but someone's mother. It was full of tears and a feeling of longing like an unabating hunger. It filled him with fear and sadness. It was like two people fighting in a long tunnel. Dream-like but somehow real. His mum always said he had a highly developed imagination. He left it at that.

It was an ordinary Saturday morning. The drone of mowers filled the air. Danny took his bike and surfboard down to the beach. It was still early and the heat had not quite arrived. A few boardies were out already. The die-hards.

The beach was his quiet place where the thoughts could stop whirling in their caged movement.

He let his bike slide down after carefully leaning his board up against the fence on the edge of the dunes. The waves were chunky in close but green glass lured out further. The tide was in and the beach was almost deserted. A couple of labs tore past, ears flying as they ran. He lay down against a dune, shading his eyes from the relentless glare of the sun on water.

He looked up watching the whiteness of gull wing disappearing into the blue, and let himself disappear into the cloud ocean above. A ship adrift. The heat sighed on his cheek and he wondered how many grains there might be in one beach.

He lay still as a rock hardly daring to breathe. The steady hush-whoosh shudder of the waves falling to the shore.

Back to school in a week. The holidays had flown by. He hated the roughness and foul mouths of most of the boys and felt so much more accepted with the girls at school. Drawn more to the Library than the playground, he was beginning to feel his separateness and differentness. It didn't help when this year he had had a loud argument with his dad about joining the Football team which he loathed with a passion. He felt totally uncoordinated, or "unco" as the kids said. "Danny Unco," they called him. He just laughed along with them but gradually had less and less of a go. Too hard. He didn't laugh when they called him a 'gaylet' though.

He was fourteen now and in his second High School year. Still felt not quite part of anything really. Just always on the fringes. An observer. A bit like how Mum feels.

'You are such a Peter Pan, Danny,' his mum said to him.

He had joked back, 'I don't think so! I hardly fly about the room wearing tights!'

His father of course had said more.

'What are ya? Jeez, I dunno. Y'head's in those art books all the time, just like your bloody mother. Fat lot of good it did her.'

Daniel had finally plucked up the courage to make his statement.

'I'm just not playing this year, Dad. I hate it.'

He did not wait for the inevitable reaction but had run out the door and gone off to the Bay.

Sometimes he felt like he hated his father. And why didn't Mum just stand up to him sometimes instead of letting him dictate and run all over her? That made him angrier than what his father was doing to her. Yet he loved his mum. Lately he felt as though she needed more from him than he could give. He sometimes felt as if he was drowning in her need to be close and be comforted.

This drowning pool held dread and fear. It made him uneasy and he wanted to withdraw from her. But that only brought more guilt. He already had enough of that with his dad, trying to live up to his expectations and never being able to. Always climbing an ice mountain. Always sliding down.

At fourteen everything was getting a different value on it. The world was turning more quickly than he wanted it to.

CHAPTER 16

The slow discernment of truth broke in by stealth, seeping in like the grey salty dawn under the bedroom curtains. The faded, blue peacock pattern had seen better days. Bob lay diagonally across the bed full of sleep and oblivion, breathing thickly.

Jenny flicked her eyes over his face, dreading to see the time ravages and the furrows edging their way down his cheeks like so much erosion. Bob O'Hare simply endured life. Gone into solitary. Jenny had lost sight of him along the way. Felt the almost physical impact of the slackened pace. Not a reflective slackening but more a hesitant divide, a fork in the road, the vehicle slowing, halting, bogged in the slow ebbing of muddied concrete.

She narrowed her eyes to slits to blur her vision, seeing him in twenty years' time. She shuddered and clenched her teeth, almost unbelieving at how clear the picture was. Bob woke startled, snuffling, almost gasping for air. The swimmer from the deep place. With the calmness of the newly-awake, he laser-gazed silently through her face, then as quickly rolled away from her to face the wall.

Something had moved inextricably between them. A shift in the tide. A movement of season, a change in the air.

Sighing, she swung her long tanned legs heavily over the side of the bed. Her head was a storm cloud. The future hung heavy, a breath held. Waiting for the second shoe to fall. She looked at the apricot-coloured wall. Such a hopeful warm colour but no longer fashionable. Throwing on her blue towelling dressing gown, she shivered at the slight chill in the air, picking up her journal and pen. April was at an end and she could honestly start to believe that summer had gasped its last.

The back garden was bursting quietly into life as well. A cheeky wagtail chittered on the fence near the kitchen window. Nothing had trespassed into the day. She stirred milk into her Darjeeling, padding down the hall with a glance into Daniel's room as she passed. The tousled sheets told her he had already gone to the surf on his bike. Probably meeting his mate Jai from down the road. She smiled as she imagined his slim little body poured into the wetsuit, his earnest expression as each wave was studied 'til the right one came along. Sliding the door open to the back yard quietly so as not to disturb Bob, she brushed past the ferns, their soft velvety fronds wet with overnight dew. She dropped down into her favourite cane chair still a little damp, positioned herself under the Lilli-Pilli. She took her first sip of tea, the best sip, watching bees begin their day in the flower beds, slim pickings now after the long hot summer.

The sentries of her mind were already admitting some of the fringe thoughts that she kept at bay at the edges, well leashed. The honest reality of her life was beginning to impact her. She opened up her journal entry from the day before.

"I am feeling truth like a revelation, a light. Feels cutting but somehow right."

She had begun a poem:

Truth, sheathed in velvet
Cuts like a blade
Opening up the portions of my life
Displayed for me
Nothing the same again.

Poetry was her secret language, a private world to escape to where she could be herself. Her journal was a cathartic exercise a lot of the time and she loved to look back at the end of the year and see where she was. Or wasn't. The fact was, she was arriving at some conclusions. The truth was, things were not OK. Another more alien feeling followed this — relief.

The calm of it landed. There came a detachment from the screenplay, and she tested the objectivity of the audience of one.

The sun climbed higher in a cloudless day. Yellow-eyed, noisy Miners clustered for the happy hour in the branches above her, dripping their lolly-pink delicacies, watching the ensuing cascade like so many jelly beans onto the grass. Such a surprise they actually tasted so bitter.

A flock of Rosellas squawked in extravagant colour flash, swamping the Bottle-brush trees at the edges of the yard; gossiping drunks in nectar bursts as the branches swayed under their collective weight.

She snapped from her reverie as the sliding door from the back room into the garden clunked back hard on its runners.

Bob rocked in the doorway, sullen and silent, as if waiting for news. Jenny drew her breath in fright, tensing her body, then deliberately let her shoulders drop, determined to enjoy her first moments of the day. She pinched her lips together, wishing him gone, wanting him far away from this new space inside her, a place as clean as the Seven Mile Beach. She saw herself on its pristine whiteness, sun blazing its white light to shimmer and mirage the horizon. The endless stretch of silver sand, the blue of hushed waves on one side and scrubby bush on the other. Her place. Her own Big Beach. A place bigger than all of them and their messy little lives. Sensing Bob's withdrawal she statued her body, until she heard the rev of the car and the gravel spluttering up from wheels.

She stood up, draining the last of the tea.

The moment stolen.

She showered quickly and dressed in jeans and T shirt. She scrawled Daniel a note, "Walking on the Seven Mile. Back soon. Love Mum."

She jumped into the old Ford Escort, heading towards the ocean and solitude.

It was as she had hoped. Deserted. Not even a fisherman around. Bob often fished the shallows when the Tailor were running. Their razor-sharp teeth were always wrecking the lines and chopping them off. The troughs and gullies fairly teemed with the silver glint of them. He'd come home recently, his bag bursting, dumping his catch in the laundry tub ready to clean and fillet. Fishing was the one passion that Bob connected with. Tide in, tide out. Dependable. No one asking any questions. Just him and the water. The horizon like a finish line.

It was early in the day with the sand cold on her bare feet as she rolled up her jeans to her knees. She liked her legs. One inheritance she could thank her mother for. Long and slender. Still in good shape from all the miles she walked in the hospital.

A few ghost crabs scuttled away as she walked down the dunes to the water, sinking up to her ankles in the soft wet sand. She began to walk out of the squelch, feeling the suck of the sand on her body. Finding herself on a solid surface, she began to walk quickly, then jog. Each pounding step seemed to clear her head and she began to think very clearly.

Thud … thud … thud. She ran without thought, moving into a zone of nothingness. Time passed. Suddenly she stopped, heart pounding and bending over to regain her breath. With no idea how long she had been running, she looked back and couldn't even see the headland of Bunjip Bay. A little frightened now and feeling very thirsty she began the long walk back.

When she returned home Daniel stood at the kitchen bench wolfing down cereal with classic adolescent appetite. He glanced up with his milk moustache grinning.

'Hi, Mum. Good walk?'

'Yeah. Yeah. How was the surf? Catch any?'

'Not bad. Dropped off though so I came home. Can you give me a lift to school?'

'Sure, Darl. Gosh, it's nearly time now. I must have walked ages!'

She hadn't run like that before and now her muscles were beginning to ache. Evening shift at the hospital tonight too. Daniel came running out, books, lunch box, drink bottle all vying for position. They left for school.

CHAPTER 17

Marilyn Bonsall flicked through the pages of the women's magazine and threw it on the floor. She leaned back on her pillows in utter boredom at the futility of her life and where she found herself. A long dry sigh broke as she winced a little as the pain returned to kick into her spine. She checked her watch hoping the next medications were due soon.

The wind picked up, stirring the needle leaves of the Casuarinas outside her window. The sound comforted her as she lay in her bed watching the clock. Listened to the tick of time. Didn't have a whole lot of that anymore. The white hum noise of the old Kelvinator, the only sound in the empty house, was familiar and assured all was as it should be. But her thoughts bore down on her like a dumping wave.

Where the heck does Richard go 'til all hours of the night these days?

He had only started this disappearing trick recently, throwing on his coat at the door.

'Gotta get some air. Back soon.'

And he was off.

She had thought a lot about Richard lately. He wasn't a particularly secretive man, quite a simplistic one really, if the truth were known. Uncomplicated, with a studied casualness she always admired. Not one to cast his eye about, so to speak. Probably not coping with this damn cancer deal.

Any more than I am, she thought.

He returned later in the night, trailing sand from the rolled up cuffs of his jeans to the shower, then to bed. These days he slept in the spare room, to give Marilyn space. Soon he'd have more space than he'd know what to do with.

Marilyn knew this new role for Richard as her carer was alien and taxing for him. But, give him his due, he was doing his level best in a no-win situation. Never one to do much in the house, having grown up as the spoilt only boy with three older sisters. With no one else vying for attention, he had never needed to do a domestic chore in his life. Marilyn had simply carried it on.

Amazingly, Richard had adapted to this new place and applied himself to the best of his ability to a task unasked for and totally unexpected to them both.

There it was.

One very small lump, almost glossed over.

And now this.

The day had dispensed its usual hot vengeance and at last the sea breeze had begun to cut through the glaze of heat lying over the town like a lid. Marilyn had become very reflective since her illness was diagnosed. Perhaps a characteristic of the dying. She seemed to have passed through the various stages of grief attributed to her condition, but was now stuck like a phonograph needle in a very monotonous groove. The long journey wearied her. She savoured the moments between the medicated oblivion and the obliteration of the long, glass-shaft of pain. Then the long-nailed bird of prey gripped her spine with its claws, rendering her unable to speak or think with any clarity.

She thought about her life. What had been done and left undone. People always said, "What would you do with your life if you knew you only had 6 months to live?" An irritating sentence, spoken by people who had their health, of course. But it swept over Marilyn's mind like the blade of a lighthouse beam. Only a little illumination to the furthest reaches of the ocean of memory, the places of no return. Treacherous reefs of shipwreck in dark places where you could run aground so easily if you lost your bearings.

Memories were dangerous places to visit. Not good to pitch your tent there. They could unwind you totally. Especially one in particular.

Guilt was her constant accompanist, hammering its black and white keys alongside her. Marilyn knew there was one place she must enter fully, to stare and regard with her eyes wide open. A place without possibilities or choices. It must happen at some point, but not today.

Now it was a time to get her affairs in order. Affairs indeed. Such a quaint old fashioned term. A time to face up and attend to the business of it all. Hadn't her mother always told her not leave a mess behind for others to clear up? She would be tidy all right. Make that will water tight. Mainly she thought of how Richard would cope with life without her in it. How he would cope with the secret she had held for too long but must now divulge.

The tears welled up easily at the thought. Life — be in it, the slogan said. Well, she wouldn't be soon.

It wasn't just the grief of losing life but the grief over never having really had it to live. Well, not in its fullness, its entirety at least. And anyway, where was her three-score-years-and-ten? So many questions and only half an answer to them all.

She threw the white pills down her throat, swallowed some water from her glass, grimacing at the bitter taste. Why did the water taste so bitter lately?

Getting all the photos in order had allowed her to enjoy the moments again. There was one black and white still in its little brown envelope lurking at the bottom of her jewellery box. She certainly wasn't ready to look at it. Not yet.

So many picnics and BBQs on the beach in those endless summers when they were all so young and beautiful and full of hope. The colours were fading in most of the photos from way back. There was one of her and Rich, the darlings of the beach set.

Richard Bonsall. Suntanned, deep brown eyes you could dive into, and that wide generous mouth always in use, laughing, talking, eating, drinking. Smiling his warmth of heart everywhere. Always the party animal, last to leave, still talking out of the car window as they drove off. Everybody's favourite.

But hers to go home with. She and Richard had been so young, so full of plans and dreams. Most dreams that would stay embryonic now. And always her Aunty Norma checking, asking her before her marriage, 'Do you want to grow old alongside this man? Together?'

Well, that won't be happening now.

They had planned a new coffee lounge for Casuarina, for all the bright young things that were beginning to congregate there, looking trendy, hoping to be seen.

Richard was the ideas person and Marilyn worked with the practicalities like money, mortgages and food on the table. Richard really had it when it came to décor and design. It was to be a coffee lounge to cater specifically for the locals particularly in the off-season, if ever there was one in Casuarina.

They dreamed of doing a big Health Food section, a new trend among the elite of the Bay. Big healthy burgers and smoothies for the army of hungry boardies who eventually beached themselves to eat. Health Food was the Next Big Thing now in trends and commerce.

The district was drawing the seekers and lookers, the city slickers looking for some bargain real estate. And now a steady stream of the lost and wayward, along with a small influx of musos, artists and photographers, all lured here by the simple life style and unspoilt beauty of the place. "The Alternatives" they were being called, along with a few other names. The local paper did a write up and one of the TV stations did a documentary on the district. Called it "Bunjip Bay: the new Byron Bay."

Sure there were similarities, but that's where it ended.

The big bucks though were mainly made in the peak season when the place was flooded with tourists and all the surfers came from everywhere to surf the Seven Mile and strut their stuff. The locals kept quiet about how many sharks there were in the area and how many actual attacks there were around the Bay. Wouldn't want to put off the tourist trade. Having them was always a love/hate relationship and most of the region was relieved when February rolled around and everyone went home 'til next time. All the Bazzas and Shazzas and Gazzas. Australian economy of speech. There were station wagons and Vee Dub Combies, all loaded with boards and bleached-blond kids, all lined up along the front studying the waves on the Seven Mile. That was before the fatalities a few years ago.

The Seven Mile where only fools and angels go, the locals said, with the surf up high and breaking at 3 metres sometimes, a green, glass slide, full of treacherous currents and hidden rips that could take the unwary out past the headland and smash them on a rock, hard and sudden. Sharks out there, too. In spite of the warning signs. Still they went out, intrepid, laughing death in the face, full of the myth of eternal youth, hoping to crack it out there.

The Japanese tourists were drawn to it like you wouldn't believe, often being swept out in rips that no local would go near, in spite of the signs in their own language.

It had been like that the day the two young surfers from Sydney came up on New Year's Eve. After a long night at the local pub boasting about their prowess at night surfing, went out with a skinful of booze, into a moonlit evening so clear you'd think you could walk on the water.

They never came back. The local surfers tried to stop them. One of them, young Chookie Thurlow, was given a fat lip for his trouble.

The Air Sea rescue searched all night and into the next day right up 'til evening when the long shadows of the scrubby trees stretched long-fingered across the beach and the only sound was the curlews calling. They were both eventually washed up further down the coast, limbs missing and barely identifiable. There were never any lifeguards on the Seven Mile as it was out-of-bounds for swimming. But still they came. The relentless pursuit of the perfect wave. A dangerous obsession.

Marilyn and Richard had married young like most of their generation. They waited one long year from the day they met. Everyone said it wouldn't last, that Richard loved the party scene too much to settle down, but Marilyn chose to ignore the hungry look she caught from time to time, as he trawled the crowd of could-be, might-bes, the new in-crowd, full of wealthy bored women looking for action and all too available.

Marilyn ignored the flirty women who gathered around him like gaudy beach butterflies at the Surf Club BBQs. While she mixed and tossed salads in the kitchen, she looked up from time to time, through the salt-encrusted windows, watching Richard in his favourite role. There he would be, the life of the party and the centre of the suntanned, beach set with their label clothes, tossing back Mateus by the glassful, throwing their heads back laughing at nothing. All white teeth and cleavage. She watched him entertaining, endlessly talking, feigning interest in them, when in truth he just wanted to be a star, to be liked and enjoyed, just for himself. The narcissus of his mirrored self, imaging what he wanted to portray, rejecting the essential man at home.

Sometimes as Marilyn floated by with trays of salad, she would catch his eye and they would exchange a conspiratorial smile. Later at home they would laugh together at the shallowness in the pool of women. She relished their closeness when it came, but recognised his need to swim out there again and again, and feel the cut of the water as it broke. She buried her fear of the hidden currents in it all, and comforted herself that it was her company he sought, her body that gave him pleasure, her nakedness he enjoyed over and over again.

If she thought about it now, she could not actually pin point when the change had come. It was probably when the diagnosis had come like a bolt from the blue. That imperceptible tide of change, when what has come in begins to go out. It was a gradual lessening of touch, of affection, of conversational sharing of gossip about friends and locals that couples always do. It was an almost indiscernible knowing, a certain boredom of expression, a sense of duty and obligation coming through the tea-making on Sunday.

There was the hope of it just being a flicker in the light, a plateau in the scheme of things. Just a temporary pause in the ebb and flow of it all. But it had been a moment. A moment of reckoning, of knowledge, as she stood one Wednesday night in the kitchen, enjoying the rosy warmth of the new overhead kitchen light, the drone of the news on TV and the last few bars of cicadas drumming as autumn began its stealthy entrance.

It had been just simple intuition or mathematics.

Making the sweet and sour sauce for the chicken sizzling in the pan, she sensed one small window in the basement of her mind letting in just enough light to see.

It was Richard's night for pool at the Surf Club, the boys' night out. His mate, Brad had rung to say it was about time Richard came to join them for a game, now that the Finals were coming up and where the hell was he?

Where the hell indeed?

Then it was simple arithmetic. Something she knew but could not quite reach, like a jar on a back shelf. What was it Brad had said? It was about time Richard joined them again … Again?

Richard had to be having an affair. And not covering his tracks very well. Simple as that. She continued stirring the sauce into the chicken and suddenly the rice boiled over flooding the stove, spitting back up at her with burning drops on her arm, snapping her back to reality. She felt she had a knowledge that was dangerous and explosive. A bomb in a brief case. She found herself going to her drawing-away place. The limpet on the rock at low tide, waiting for a new wave. She rolled the information around, a marble in a bowl, testing the truth against the fiction.

She heard the familiar sound of the key in the front door and composed her face.

'Hi, Darl. Dinner ready? I'm off out tonight.'

'Yep. Won't be a sec.'

She averted her face as he went to kiss her, concentrating hard on the sauce congealing on the stove, almost too anxious to not divulge.

'Oh by the way, Brad rang. Wants to know if you'll be there tonight. Something about the Finals coming up I think he said?'

She watched his face closely as the tiny, animal flick of fear slid through his eyes, then went to ground.

He turned his back.

'Yeah. Yeah. OK. Can't let the boys down. Just get changed.'

A tight knot of steel formed in her stomach. A numbness came as a shock wave hit her. She dished up the meal too fast, too angrily, smashing the serving spoon so hard it cracked Richard's plate. It fell apart in a neat line straight across.

Careful, she said to herself. You have no proof of anything.

But I don't need it.

CHAPTER 18

It was the unusual movement of the torchlight that grabbed Jenny's eye. They were flashes like signalling. From where she sat, high up on the top of the dunes at the Seven Mile, Jenny could see the whole reach of the beach, its conch-shell echoes of ocean pounding the shore, soft to hard.

A flicker. A definite flicker. Not the fixed gas-lamp glare of the fishermen knee-deep in the gullies, hauling in the tailor as they schooled past in silver scuds. It was the movement of light that attracted her attention. The unusual arc of splintered light. Probably just a kid with his dad down fishing. The sort of thing Danny would do with Bob, when he was bored with all the endless waiting. He and Bob used to do a lot of night fishing once, but it seemed both had lost interest in doing much at all together these days.

Sometimes Bob would come down on his own when the fish were really on, go off after the yabbies in the late afternoon then take the bait and rods down later on at sundown. The best fishing times always seemed so inopportune to normal life.

The sky was a velvet canopy with a bit of stardust sprinkled around tonight. Jenny had come round the headland to the Seven Mile, its shadowy vastness stretching away, a bolt of shot silk rolled out under the moonlight.

She had left the house early tonight. Bob had begun to beer up earlier these days and had slumped asleep before nine. Not as aggressive any more but still always there just under the surface.

Danny had taken to spending as much time as possible with his mate, Jai, only a few houses away. The house had become thick with the atmosphere of unspoken words. The beach was her escape now, with its silent clean sweeps. Here she was able to release the fringe thoughts off their tight leash for a run. She began to face the truth that she really did not want to be in the same room as her husband any more, but felt powerlessly incapable of expressing it, even to herself. She had no idea what to do. There was no way she was about to visit Bernadette and run the risk of being persuaded out of what she truly felt.

She felt the subtle distancing. The edginess. Too many gaps now.

The sand was hard and cold beneath the bones of her hips, but she stayed despite the discomfort. She watched the great sky-show of clouds gathering, partially obscuring the moon now, galleons voyaging across the sky. She watched fascinated as the torch dancer arced his light, seeming to go from one fisherman to the next, stopping briefly to chat as he moved along the beach. As she strained to see the moonlit beach she realised it was not the figure of a child but a man.

How weird. What was he doing here? Just some weirdo, I guess. The Bay is full of them. Who cares?

And she leaned back on her dune chair, the cool sand pillow, knowing the fine grains would be in her ears and her hair which would now need a wash before bed. She drifted down into a light sleep, tired after three nights straight at the hospital. She woke to the sound of a man singing. Singing quite loudly now, the arc of his torch approaching quite quickly.

Chapter 18

'Sweet Car O-line ... nah ... nah ... nah...'

Jenny shrank into the dune alarmed now, angry at the intrusion. She felt the old familiar fear, watching his approach up the steep dune with large steps. Sure he could see her now backed into a curve in the sand, her whole body stiffened as she held her breath. The moon cast dappled light across the dune. The torch swung its rhythm in his hand, keeping beat to the song he was singing. But in a moment he had passed. She caught a glimpse of jeans rolled up and a check flannelette shirt hanging out. The town uniform. He ran wildly over the dunes like a child, up one and down another, waving the torch in demented arcs along the top of the dunes.

Jenny pulled herself up with a mixture of fear and annoyance. Her space had been invaded.

'What an idiot.'

Sand had run almost into her eyes and the edges of her mouth and she brushed it off as best she could, irritated at his intrusion into her stolen solitude. She ran to the car parked on the bitumen edge in the car park under the single light next to the fishermen's rust buckets. After shaking out sand from the cuffs of her jeans, out of her hair and her shirt sleeves, she unlocked the car, and flung herself in, revving the car too hard. It spluttered and the motor flooded. Waiting in the dark cabin, the air rank with petrol fumes, her anxiety turned to fear for no real reason. She locked the car, shaking a little but determined to settle down. After what seemed an eternity she tried the ignition again. It sprang to life.

She moved off, out of the car park, down past the estuary, dark now — never any street lights. She rounded the corner out of the Estuary road into her street, Jacaranda Avenue. Most of the house lights were out with just an odd porch light on, its arc of yellow illuminating the usual pot plants in assembled profusion on the front.

Her own house was swallowed by darkness right through to the back door. It felt abandoned and empty. Her hands trembled a little as she went to open the front door. It was locked. No one ever locked the doors around here, it was such sleepy-hollow place.

She made her way down the side of the house, falling over debris and knocking over the wheel barrow and a couple of paint tins as she went, feeling her way in the dark passage alongside the house. Somewhere near a dog barked in alarm. The bricks of the walls of the house still felt warm from the day's sun. Creatures scuttled in the vegetation beside the side fence. The Bandicoots were already in the garden tunnelling through the moist earth like so many moles. Cane toads moved clumsily out of her way with solid wet splats.

Calmer now, she opened the sliding door, without catching it on its runners. It was unlocked and partially open. She crept into the kitchen which open-planned into the lounge room, then put on the overhead stove light and looked across to Bob's old, brown vinyl recliner. Bob snored loudly, splayed across the lounge, newspapers covering every surface of him, the floor and furniture. Empty brown stubbies littered the floor. With a thankfulness that surprised her, she turned out the lights, trailing sand to the bathroom.

Under the warm shower, the water washed away the night. An unease fluttered in her belly at the memory of the singing man with the torch. Neil Diamond in the sand hills.

Safe now in her own house she smiled now at the recollection.

Leaving Bob out in the lounge she slept alone in the wide bed. Bob snored away the night surrounded by his own detritus.

CHAPTER 19

'Mum.'

'Hmm?'

The blond thatch. The blue trust of little-boy eyes. Danny leaned over her from behind her chair, kneading her shoulder with his chin, as he had done since he was tiny. She relaxed into the old pattern of affection but knew too that he wanted something important.

'Can I go to the Drag Races with Jai on Sat'day night? And sleep over? Please Mum?'

'Maybe. I'll talk to Dad.'

Danny recoiled, drawing back from her.

'He'll say no for sure. Don't worry about it.'

'But Danny...'

He was gone, already running down the side of the house. She heard his noisy exit through the rubble down the side passage. The wheelbarrow still lay where she'd knocked it over in the night. The gravel ripped as he pedalled off on his bike. She walked to the window, looking down the long driveway flanked by Poincianas, their vibrant red flowers staggering to the end of their season. Daniel was a flash of blue as he rounded the end of the drive and onto the main road. She prayed a silent prayer of protection as he cycled out of sight.

'This is no good. Something has to change.'

She'd longed to have had a little girl as well. Bob had been adamant. No more babies.

Her mind often floated back to the pain of the loss through miscarriage of all those little lives. A miscarriage of justice. Until Danny came along. Everything different. For a while at least. Sometimes Jenny's arms ached with a longing to hold another child again. Still. It's not too late. You never know what might happen. I hate what's happening to Danny though. I'll have to talk to Bob. And maybe spend some time with Danny. Except he's getting past that now and would rather be with Jai. Of course.

She went back into the kitchen and got out all the ingredients for Chocolate Brownies. Danny's favourite. Sure to be a winner.

CHAPTER 20

Pastor Kevin Blake was a small unassuming man with limited expectations and a strong desire to be safe in his life. He fulfilled his duties as a pastor at a local church that was largely uninspiring and small in congregational numbers. He gave the impression of smallness, neatness and discretion and of being neutral in colour from his hair to his plain, brown lace up shoes. He had been a scholarly man, but had settled with resignation and some relief into his post at the Casuarina Bay Family Life Church. He had been there now for some 25 years and had earned the trust of the town. He had listened to their grievances and angers, their confessions of lust and attempted murder, which, for a small town such as Casuarina, had been reasonably plentiful, but he remained the epitome of confidentiality.

His wife, Janice, had settled into quiet resignation as befitted the wife of a country pastor and suited him admirably. Now with greying hair, she had it set and coloured once a month at the local hairdressers and considered that to be splurge enough. They had thrown open their house and their church building during that dreadful cyclone of '77, and the townspeople had never forgotten it. Both teetotallers, their two daughters had gone off to the city to become Primary school teachers. They lived out their unremarkable and unassuming lives simply doing their role.

Kevin Blake was not a man to rock the boat or ruffle the feathers of the town's society in whatever strata it was found. Some would term him a "yes man," but he preferred to see himself as a man for all seasons, a friend to most. An inoffensive little man, his hair greying now in what had been a full head of raven black hair, small in features and stature, he carefully closed the door of his discreet, grey early-model sedan and walked with some hesitation up the driveway of the high-set Western Red cedar house and up the steps to the front veranda.

The Casuarinas whispered their secrets to the Poinciana, its shade spreading outwards and downwards almost to the ground.

The house had a closed attitude about it, all the curtains drawn against the sun, the thick silence resisting the intrusion of the day. He was not surprised to get the call from his secretary, summoning him here on this day. So many times people were referred to him from the Hospital Chaplaincy, where he presided as president. Many asked for his involvement with home visits to those who had been diagnosed with a terminal illness. He placed himself in neutral gear and straightened his shoulders.

He was surprised to find the weathered front door ajar. It came open with little resistance. Immediately he heard the slow-paced click-click of dog claws across old lino. An ageing and arthritic Labrador came wagging towards him in greeting. Pastor Kevin bent down to pat the old yellow head. Down the darkened hallway he could hear the faint strains of instrumental music playing.

He adjusted his eyes to the gloom of the interior, a sudden contrast to the glare of the outside. Then he peered back out along the long, covered wooden veranda with its faded decking, a few old canvas chairs spaced at intervals along it. Right at the end of the long veranda was a striped outdoor lounge and it took him a moment or two to distinguish the small shape of a woman lying on it, with one arm trailing on the floor. He turned away from the open door and called out softly so as not to startle her. Marilyn woke from a deep place and reached for her sheet that had fallen off onto the floor. She sat upright too quickly and sank back immediately onto the pillows .

'Sorry to startle you. I'm Kevin Blake, you rang my office ... last week ... you know, for today? Hospital chaplain...' His voice trailed off.

She gradually focused and began to sit up, motioning to him that she could manage without help.

'Yes ... yes of course ... I'm so sorry ... I forgot ... I'm Marilyn ... Marilyn Bonsall. Thank you for coming so quickly ... I, I just needed to talk to somebody about, about...'

Kevin's soothing voice relaxed her as he looked round in the gloom for something to sit on, less a place to sit as something to bring him down to her level on the lounge.

'Look, let's go inside to the lounge, it's easier in there. Can I make you some tea? Coffee?'

Kevin waved his hand in dismissal of the offer. Marilyn allowed him to help her from the lounge but once upright she made her way along the veranda wall unaided. The old yellow Lab who had flung himself down at the end of the veranda rose and dutifully followed them inside. Marilyn took her time to get to the front door and then inside to the hallway. She held on to the wall and crept along at a snail's pace. Her breathlessness, which had only come on in the last few days, frightened her. She led the way to the lounge room and to a comfortable apple-green, fabric recliner where with some effort and a painful groan, she managed to lower herself, and adjust the lever at the side and spread her small frame along the length of it.

The room was tastefully decorated in cream and brown tones, cream carpet and chocolate-brown lounges with cushions in different shades of red strewn along them. There were various pastel-coloured Gaugin prints on the walls. The whole room had a feeling of comfort and light. There was no clutter on shelves or tables. On one wall was a painting of the Seven Mile, done by a local artist. Pastor Blake recognised the distinctive style. He went to comment then changed his mind.

He sat down opposite her and waited for her to catch her breath and begin to speak. He didn't have to wait long. She turned her once beautiful face with its sunken almost black eyes framed now in a scarf because of hair loss, and looked him straight in the eye.

'See – I don't really believe all this God stuff. Well, not the way other people do. I'd like to, you know, believe in an afterlife and everything. I mean, I feel I should...' her voice trailed off almost apologetically.

Kevin leaned forward. This was his cue, his familiar place. He looked at the sad gaunt face, the despair and fear, and desperately wanted to say something of weight and of value, that might lift the burden somehow.

'Marilyn, let me ask you something. Do you believe in the wind?'

'What do you mean?'

'You believe in the wind because you can feel the effects of it, a gentle breeze, a strong gust of it, even a cyclone.'

'But you can't actually see the wind.'

'Precisely so. God is the same. Only believe.'

As if in agreement, two doors slammed in quick succession, as a sudden unexpected gust slammed against the house, rattling the blinds along the veranda. They smiled at one another in a moment of complete understanding.

Marilyn lay back in the recliner, coughing a little, breathless now, but feeling a release like a bird long held captive in a cage too small. She lifted herself on one elbow, pleading into his face.

'I need to tell you … tell someone ... something I have never told anyone. Not even Richard knows. Before I … go.'

Kevin relaxed. The last confessions of the dying. As if they needed to leave without baggage to the next destination.

He looked at her face attentively. 'Go on.'

'Well, it was a long time ago now. I was nineteen and I'd had way too much to drink. It was a one-off really but … there was a baby. A girl. Richard and I ... well we never had any luck in that department. So sad. I gave her away. Adopted her out at birth.'

She began to cry, the tears running in streams down her face, her body shaking with repressed grief and loss.

Kevin patted her arm and sighed. 'Did the father ever know?'

'Yes, but I went away to Sydney and had her there. I never spoke about it again.' Her eyes widened. 'Richard has no idea. Please...'

'Don't worry. I have a big hat. Lots of secrets under there.' He tapped his head, and smiled in conspiracy.

'It was someone you may know. Bob O'Hare. Looked so like him with those dark eyes and hair. I saw her. Held her. Before they took her away, I mean. We were young and it was just a fling. But I think of her every day. Particularly now. '

Compassion swept over Kevin as he struggled to find the words. He didn't need to. The freedom of confession was a universal experience. Nothing surprised him anymore. He knew Bob slightly, but only as a loud-mouth drunk with a sweet wife and son.

'Could we ... could you ... sort of say something or could we... ? I need to finalise...'

A coughing spasm overtook her and she fell back exhausted.

Kevin's face crinkled with the smile lines of many moments just like this. Realising the poignancy of this moment, he took her limp hand in his own two and began to say a prayer. Marilyn closed her eyes, her lips a little apart, and drank in the words washing over her, nodding in agreement with him. Relaxing now, sleep, which had evaded her like warmth in the cold, began to envelop her tired mind.

Kevin got up quietly, patting the dog on his way past. The old dog thumped his tail in approval as he lay next to Marilyn's chair, his tongue lolling loosely, not attempting to see him out. He knew his role.

The afternoon was beginning to draw in. He opened the car door, leaning back heavily in the driver's seat. He started the engine as quietly as he could and sighing deeply, drove off.

For the first time in a long time Marilyn slept a dreamless and uninterrupted sleep.

CHAPTER 21

Richard was particularly edgy that Thursday morning. Guilt, the great revealer of heart motives, ruled the patterns of his life. He took extra care with Marilyn's tray, reaching over the veranda rail to pick a cluster of pale pink Bougainvillea from the vine that covered the whole front of the old Queenslander.

He placed it next to her orange juice with a single piece of buttered kibble-wheat toast, and a couple of slices of mango. Her favourite breakfast at the moment. The pink blossoms grew on the vine now in great profusion, their long green thorns a trap for unwary fingers. He remembered buying her the plant years ago for her birthday. It had been a few inches tall in a pot and now, it almost obscured the light. A remembered tenderness returned for a moment, the memory of times past, good times, but times that had slipped away on some tide somewhere, and gone out to sea.

He couldn't remember when he had stopped wanting her, to touch her, even just to hold her hand. In the beginning the diagnosis had shocked him, then repulsed him. He was afraid of her body, of hurting, of catching something, making it worse somehow. Interesting word, diagnosis, "through knowing".

Dealing with the guilt at his own response had been harder than looking at the reality of the disease prognosis. Such a full stop. Cancer happened to other people, not to us. To her. He raged at the sky, at God, at life. Walking on that vast sand at night sometimes he felt he was crying for his own lack, his own losses, his missed opportunities. He felt it unfair that Marilyn was fading like an old photo in the sun while he gained strength. He feared the pain she held and feared his own pain at the loss of all she had ever been to him. It caused a great chasm. An unspeakable need for both of them. Was it some sort of karma or payback for all his lack? All the women he'd just glanced at, but never more than that?

Give him his due, he'd been faithful right to the last. A one-woman man. Remembered that sea of gorgeous women in the surf club days, breasts almost tumbling out of their enclosed spaces like escaped melons. He knew that Maz saw it all.

'Hey Rich! Rich! Eyes up, Darling!'

'Honey, Honey,' he would say to her, 'look, just because a man looks doesn't mean he wants. OK? You'll always be enough for me.' And they had laughed together, secure in the knowing.

Now they were beginning to release each other in different ways and for different reasons. A more permanent detachment.

He'd had a chat to the Palliative Care nurse about the end and even the funeral. It all seemed too clinical to Richard. Nice girl and all. Jenny, her name was. Last time he saw her she looked like she had a shiner. Who'd do that to a woman?

Richard had begun to disappear in the evenings, finding the house stifling and claustrophobic, its heavy silence engulfing. He knew it was blatantly selfish but felt powerless to cope with what lay ahead.

He jumped into the old Ute and drove like a bat out of hell to the Seven Mile where only the fishermen and the sea co-existed. He found a release in its freshness, its quiet dependable presence, tides in, tides out. Something you could rely on. He enjoyed chatting to the fishermen as they stood in their waders, great boots attached to rubber overalls that kept them dry during their long vigil on the edge of hope. He watched them try their luck, taciturn and solitary, exercising their patience. A breed alone, the night fisherman. Escapism in some ways. Not really his scene though. Sometimes he would ask the customary question, 'Any bites, mate?'

They were men of few words, concentrating on the line tension, the waves and tides coming in, how far up the beach the tackle was, adjusting torches, re-baiting the lines.

One night he asked one of the fishermen who was standing up to his waist in the waves about why some of them wore waders when it was so shallow. This one had none on.

Concentrating on his line, and walking backwards out of a small gully, he turned to Richard and said, 'Nah, mate. I don't believe in 'em meself. A bloke'd be mad to go out any further into them gullies out there wearin' them bloody things. There's deep gullies out there and one wave and you're over. Boots fill up with water and you're gone. Just like that. I'd never wear 'em.' He snorted and spat into the water.

Richard tired of the limited conversation with the men. After all they were there to get away from people and do some serious fishing. He preferred to go higher up the beach, taking his torch with him, up into the tops of the high dunes where no one ever went. Well, certainly not at night, anyway.

Except the other night. Felt sure someone was up there in one of those chair-shaped dunes way up above the beach and out of the wind. That was the night he felt like singing. A little uncharacteristic, even for him.

It wasn't that he could see anyone really, more of a sensing that someone was very near him in the darkness there, and that he was being watched.

Usually Richard returned from the Seven Mile, windswept and salty, sand spilling out of clothes humming and singing, as he washed off the salt and sand at the tap at the back steps. Feeling the freedom, the space.

At nine o'clock one Tuesday evening the shrill tone of the telephone pierced the silence of the Bonsall's darkened house.

Richard was out and Marilyn felt too weak to reach the other room where the phone was. She heard the click of the answering machine and her own familiar voice from healthier days, bright and positive, inviting the caller to leave a message.

'Marilyn! Marilyn! Is that you, Dear? Pick it up if you're there, Dear! It's Aunty Norma here. I'm coming up from Sydney, be there tomorrow, and don't worry I'll find my own way. OK, Dear, see you soon."

Hot tears stung her eyes. She let them course down her face as she heard the familiar nasal twang of the only woman who had been there for her throughout her life.

Aunty Norma. Bastion of all that was dependable and motherly. Aunty Norma, overweight and loud to match, a no-nonsense woman, her great bulk swathed in polyester and gold chains around her neck all lost in the flab of her overgenerous neck and chin all spilling over in the laughter she shook in. She was the essence of stoic forbearance. A no-frills woman with a soldiering mentality to push on and push through whatever calamities life proffered.

It was Aunty Norma who had been there for eight-year-old Marilyn when her Mum and Dad along with that other couple were killed instantly at the level-crossing smash on their way to a wedding in Sydney. It suddenly rendered Marilyn an orphan. The tragedy shook the town. Aunty Norma had arrived, having now lost her only sister. Shelving her own grief, she brought with her an atmosphere of normality in the chaos that ensued, as Marilyn and her aunt clung to each other in their mutual pain. Marilyn remembered how as a little girl her aunt had shielded her from the pitying looks of the town, the furtive glances and whispered asides as she buried her face in the bosomy pillow of acceptance that was Aunty Norma. They needed each other.

It was shortly after that they moved to Casuarina Bay, away from the Sydney suburbs, away from the pain and the memories. It was a place where Marilyn was able to start again, with the open windy beach and her first very own Labrador puppy to ease her through it all. Until the baby, that is.

Aunty Norma was not quite so understanding about that. Her face drained of colour when Marilyn, expecting sympathy, found detachment and disapproval, as she realised that respectability was high on Aunty Norma's list of essentials.

'Starting to show a bit now, Love. Best we send you down to Sydney 'til it's over.'

It would never be over. She thought back to the quiet ivy-covered walls of the Convent in Sydney, where twenty-three other teenage mothers were secreted, away from the prying gaze of the general public.

Aunty Norma gave her one last enveloping hug, and with a resolute face, turned quickly and walked away from the iron gate at the entrance to the Convent. It had a sort of hospital feel to it, smells of disinfectant and boiled cabbage wafted into the hallway.

A thin wiry woman with a closed face appeared from nowhere, sizing her up. 'I'm Matron Burgess,' she said, pursing her lips in a disapproving line. 'You are Marilyn? We don't use last names here. Bring your bag.' She walked off down the long hallway that had closed doors on each side. Metal name tag holders were screwed into each door. The Matron stopped in front of a door at the end of the corridor. 'You're in with Patty. She's our youngest. Fourteen.' She walked off leaving Marilyn outside the closed door, case in hand. As she got to the end of the corridor she turned round, hands on hips. 'Lunch is at twelve. Don't be late.' And disappeared around the corner.

Marilyn slowly opened the door which resisted with a squeak. No one there. There were two single beds with faded pink chenille bedspreads on them. A small wooden chest of drawers with a few handles missing sat was against one of the brick walls. A porcelain statue of Mary with halo and hands extended, looking up to heaven, was the only adornment in the room. It was for all the world, a cell. She flopped on the bed with a sigh, propping herself and her beachball belly with her arms behind her. She squeezed her eyes tight, fighting back tears.

They were cheap slave labour at the nearby hospital, staggering under the load of laundry baskets and doing twelve-hour split shifts in the kitchen, ankles swollen and bellies enormous as their time drew near.

Remembered the loneliness and boredom of the bare brick room with its small hard bed and no window. The silent nuns whooshing past in the highly polished hallway, heads down, off to prayer. The faint hum of traffic on the other side of the high brick walls, the real world. Forbidden to leave the premises. The girls gathered in little shameful clumps, whispering, knowing they could never take their babies home. No one talked about their baby. No one spoke of how they really felt.

The excruciating pain of the birth with no medications, the sly snippet from the old, dried-prune nurse, 'You'll think about it next time you want to play up, won't you?'

She lost a few days after that, in a Pentabarb cloud of oblivion. To "help her recover".

That's when she signed the form.

'This is just to register the birth, Dear,' lied a social worker with a face like flint. Little did she know they were the adoption papers in her drugged stupor.

She signed.

Father: unknown. What a lie. She barely remembered Bob O'Hare's hot breath and fumbling in the dark on the beach towel at the Seven Mile. The smell of engine grease that she hated to this day. It was over before it began. Then three missed periods. And now here it was. Or rather, she.

The welfare woman was brusque and cold in her grey suit and sensible creaky black shoes. She spoke into the middle distance above Marilyn's head

'It's best this way. A clean break. You can't bring a child up. Got a happily married couple waiting for this one. It'd be selfish to want to keep it, wouldn't it?'

Her little black-haired girl with the dark eyes was whisked off to somewhere else. She never saw her again.

After she came back to town and the adoption had gone through, she found herself avoiding the places that Bob would frequent. The following summer she ran into him at a Surf Club party. He never even asked. In that moment she hated him. He looked, then looked away and slunk off straight away.

After every summer season she noticed the absence of a couple of the teenage girls. The Morris girl went away two years in a row.

Richard seemed to come into her life just at the right time. No babies though. They had talked about it at the beginning but Marilyn had never felt she could share her deepest secret with him.

After two years of trying for a baby Richard was philosophical about it all, 'Never mind love. We've got each other, hey. Some women just can't have babies, can they?'

She longed to hold a baby of their own but somewhere along the line she buried her deepest desire in a cavern.

Two days after the Reverend Blake had visited, Richard came in with a brown envelope for her. On the front was written, "Private and confidential." She already sensed what it was.

'Later.' She whispered to the air as she placed it in the pocket of her dressing gown.

CHAPTER 22

Jenny sat at the wheel of her car, tears plopping onto her lap. She punched the steering wheel 'til it vibrated. Her head was still zinging from the blow she didn't see coming. She had been stupid to dismiss the heavy clunk of glass on glass as Bob reached for the third time into his hidden stash at the back of the veranda cupboard. The clink gave it away though. Whisky. Should've left then.

She saw the rage and fire in his eyes as he lunged towards her knocking her into the door frame. No shift at the hospital tonight. Danny had gone to bed early, thank God. She could hear the tranny music coming from his room. Locked these days. It had been just her and Bob at home, skirting around each other like a couple of snarly dogs. It had been over the usual nothing, but this time Jenny knew she had some decisions to make.

Heard the snap of the screen door and without looking over her shoulder ran to the car. Still shaking, she drove down the dark driveway and into the sleeping town. She wound the window down at the Seven Mile car park and felt the breath of salty wind on her cheek.

The old Ute that she had seen before was parked at the far end. Opening her door, she grabbed a torch from the glove box, along with some chewy. She trudged across the windswept beach and up into the dunes where it was quiet. Darkness dropped down on her like a welcome cloak.

It was more an awareness of a light than the actuality of it that caused her to spin around, her torch spilling in an arc across the sky space. In the final seconds of light spooling she caught sight of a figure walking fast across the top where the trees started. Sometimes the roos would come out of the bush, leaping across like prehistoric creatures in moonlight. She held her breath, listening. Then it was unmistakable.

'Sweet Caroline ... nuh ... nuh ... nuh...'

It was the loony guy from before. She made her shoulders relax and sat up near the top of a dune, watching around her, the torch switched on. Senses on high alert. The sound increased.

He came closer and stopped. Stumbled backwards and fell tumbling to the bottom of the dune. She heard him swear softly.

'Good God! What are you doing up here?'

He climbed heavily up the dune, puffing as he reached the top. She shone the torch on his face. Like a rabbit in the spotlight, he stood, hands on hips, flanno fluttering like a torn flag in the wind.

Jenny put the torchlight somewhere between them both, getting on her haunches, ready to run if needed.

'I might ask you the same thing.'

He seemed familiar, but it was a fairly dark night with the moon obscured by leaden cloud.

Richard Bonsall crouched down. 'D'you mind if I sit for a minute?'

Jenny moved over slightly. 'Look. I'm really not...'

'Yeah, I know. Sorry. Didn't mean to be rude. It's just I, I need to get away sometimes. My wife's sick. Actually, she's dying. Cancer. In the bones now.'

He looked down not sure how to go on. It seemed like an explanation of his singing presence.

Jenny put her invisible nurse hat on. 'I'm a nurse. I look after a lot of cancer patients. It's hard for you, isn't it?'

Richard breathed in deeply and sat down near her. He glanced sideways in the torchlight.

'Hang on. I've met you. The other week. You were really...'

Jenny sighed, her head on one side. She touched the throbbing lump on her head, suddenly exhausted.

'Yes,' she said more softly. 'You did.'

'I don't know what to say to her. She hasn't got long. I don't cope like I should. So I walk. Here.' He patted the sand next to him.

The moon peeped out from the cloud mass and the dune was suddenly illuminated. The silver grass waved its arms. Moonlight bathed her face like the bruise that was now emerging. They looked at each other for a long moment.

'What's happened to your face? It's all swollen and your eye ... who did this to you? You're running away, aren't you?'

Jenny picked up a stick and made figure eights in the sand. Looked at him and then away. She saw a tall gaunt man with chiselled features and dark curly hair falling across his forehead.

The silence hung between them. Jenny just wanted space and time alone. She got up slowly and started to walk down the dune. She sank quickly into sand up to her knees but reached the bottom quickly. The beach shone wetly as the tide launched itself into coming to shore. She began to run away from the town, her feet thudding on the hard wet sand. Her head throbbed .

In a few minutes she heard snatches of his voice over the crash of waves.

'Wait. Wait up ... sorry ... I didn't mean to...'

It was inevitable. Jenny slowed, puffing, hands on hips.

'Look, I don't feel like company tonight. You're right. I am running away. My life is awful and I have a lot of decisions to make.'

'Can I just walk a little way with you then?'

She shrugged. 'Suit yourself.'

They walked in silence together along the shore, their feet glumphing in the wet sand, scattering crabs as they went. It was almost companionable as they each began to relax a little. The darkness helped.

Jenny felt safe with him.

'I saw you up there a few weeks ago.'

She stopped mid-stride and with a faint smile said, 'Do you come here often?'

He grinned back. 'Yeah. Fairly.'

He patted his chest twice. 'Richard,' he said.

'I'm Jenny. And I do remember you. Look, as far as your wife goes, just be yourself. Tell her how you feel. Got nothing to lose, hey?' Good God, I am counselling a man about his wife's death, after midnight. On a beach. In the dark. Too ridiculous.

She turned back towards the faint lights of Bunjip Bay.

'It's late. I have to work tomorrow. Gotta get this lump down before then. Maybe we can talk another time. See ya.'

She began the homeward stretch, then turned into Caroline's street where she could already see the porch light was on.

CHAPTER 23

Marilyn turned the brown envelope over and over in her hands. If I open it, everything will change. She drummed her fingers on the table and thought back to the day her baby girl was taken away. Seeing the downy dark hair on her perfect little head.

The secrecy. The shame. And always, always the wondering what had become of her. In her mind, her baby was always called Rachel. She thought of her most days, and on her birthday every year had bought a card and written in it along with a bunch of flowers in honour of her memory. September was always the season for daffodils and jonquils. Their smell always reminded her of her little girl.

She looked at the back of the envelope which only stated that it had been sent by a government department. Impulsively, her hand trembling, she ripped the envelope opened. She began to read:

"Dear Mrs. Bonsall, we have been instructed by our client to attempt to get in touch with you. According to the hospital records you gave birth to a baby girl on September 5th of 1967..."

She fell back on the pillows.

'Why now?'

The tears came suddenly. She read the letter again. After all these years. She wants to know me, meet me. I haven't got long, I know that. Reaching for the pain killers she sank back onto the pillows, no longer caught in indecision but knowing what she most wanted and what had to be done. Every secret finds its way out. Eventually. No time to lose now.

The sun was a red slash along the line of the veranda when Richard came home. The dog looked up, tail thumping.

Richard went over to where Marilyn was lying. 'Hey, Mazzie. What can I get you?'

She waved him off with her hand and hauled up on one elbow. 'Richard. There's something I need you to know. It's time.'

Richard stepped back a pace, thoughts tumbling. A slight freeze of fear tingled his brain. He stepped forward to where his wife lay, vulnerable and frail. He stretched out his arms.

'Come on. Let's get you up and go into the lounge. I'll make us some tea. Peppermint?'

She let him lift her from the recliner and leaned into his warmth. It had been a long time.

CHAPTER 24

Dawn comes flamingo pink etching the great sky with promise for the day. Another hot one by the look. The sea is diamond bright lolling about lazily, waiting for the tide to turn with resolution.

The body of the man is large and inert, the waders filling with the oncoming tide causing the lower legs to float in the water incongruously like a blow up figure. The arms are splayed abroad for all the world like a man surrendered to the elements. A cluster of seagulls gathers respectfully nearby, observing.

Bob O'Hare lies sprawled across the shallows on the Seven Mile. His mouth is a void of purple entry as the water gushes in and out at will, his face a mottled grey. One nostril is entirely buried in the wet sand. Floating near his right hand are several fifty-dollar notes. Sand crabs scuttle about. Business as usual. No one is on the beach. Not even an early fisherman.

The knock at the door is soft and unsure. It's early. Just past dawn. A uniformed policeman stands resolutely on the doormat, his face set but soft. As Jenny approaches the door she sees through the coloured glass it's the same policeman who attended Caroline's house that time she needed help. She'd know those freckles anywhere. She doesn't like him already.

The shock hits her like a brick in the guts. She reels like a drunk against the wall.

Her voice trails off as her mind, whirling with a thousand thoughts tries to grasp the news. She hears Danny stirring in his room. The tranny is a low hum. It's taking forever for words to form.

'My God I didn't even hear him leave the house…'

'What? What is it Mum?'

He emerges, yawning and sleepy, a puzzled look on his face. She goes to him, hands to her face, wide eyes.

'It, it's your father. He's been found on the beach. Drowned. I have to go down to see.'

She's shaky now as truth begins to hit. And hits. She dials Caroline's number.

CHAPTER 25

"Body of Fisherman Found on Seven Mile Beach" was the headline in the Tribunal. A life unlived to its full potential. Or not.

For the second time in Jenny's life death hit home. But all her father had got was a two line mention on page four of the local rag. Sadness swept over her as she remembered coming back to the house she had left behind so many years before, her father's small body being removed by the ambos, nobody looking at anyone else or saying anything at all. "No suspicious circumstances" the paper said. This time and the time before. Suspicion was hardly the word. Circumstances, yes.

Bob's funeral took a while to arrange. First there was a Coroner's inquest but no foul play was suspected. Foul Play. Hardly play at all. And what do you wear to your husband's funeral, for heaven's sake? In the end she opted for the burgundy suit with the cream high-necked blouse under it. Fitting, really.

They went through the motions of doing the right thing. Pastor Kevin Blake arrived at the house, a calm and sensible presence. He sat out on the veranda chairs with Danny and took time talking him through what had happened.

Caroline came and stayed the night, helping Jenny with who to inform, making phone calls, finding addresses. Bernadette dropped in a beef casserole along with a dozen clichés along the lines of all things working together for good. Fair enough.

A deep peace and what she could only acknowledge as relief, crested on the house.

The day of the funeral was clear and bright. A new day dawning with a promise of more to come. Bob's two sisters attended in grim silence. Dark currant eyes darting about like busy blow flies. Jenny hadn't seen them since their mother's funeral all those years ago. Left as quickly as they arrived, saying not a word to Jenny. Nothing had changed.

It was done. And dusted.

A few people came back to the house for tea and sandwiches, in a half-hearted attempt to show respect to Bob. The sisters didn't bother The wind whipped around the house, chasing dead leaves and papers down the side passage.

After they all left Daniel threw himself on the lounge and switched on the telly, engrossing quickly. The strident notes of the Bonanza opening theme music filled the lounge room. The rest of the house was silent and empty in a new way. Jenny wandered through, collecting the detritus of one man's failed life. She gathered up clothes, empty beer bottles, newspapers and dirty socks, shoving them into empty beer cartons, not daring to exhale in this new space of choice.

Carefully closing the door where Danny was watching his programme, she began to cull. Every unnecessary and stupid collected article over a span of years, piled together in the corner of the lounge room. Felt her arms and legs energised, but not belonging to her. Piled up all the collections of home magazines, women's magazines, unread books and Bob's old engine parts and ashtrays, all piled together. Fury building like the tide coming in.

Chapter 25

She's in a frenzy now, hurling and smashing everything she sees in the room. Casts her eye on the Noritake tea set, the only thing Bob's Mum ever gave them. A wedding present. She'd always hated it with its prissy little white daisies on the green china, and too-small cup handles. Bob always treated it like the holy grail and no one was ever allowed to touch it.

She wrenches open the glass sideboard door, cups cascading onto each other, smashing onto the floor. Her eyes light on the framed photo of her and Bob, a rare shot taken of them down at the beach before Danny came along. Her face, framed in her long blond hair, smiling and hopeful. And Bob, scowling and frowning, gaunt and dark, even then. She picks up the frame and smashes it down on the wooden coffee table where it splinters into pieces. Reaching through the glass she feels the welcome pain of cut flesh, then grabs the old photo in both hands. The blood is streaming from her hand. Lets the pain of disappointment and rage fill her mouth with its toxins, along with the dry metallic taste of blood as she puts her hand to her lips.

Suddenly the door opens and Danny is standing there, horrified at the scene in front of him.

'Mum! What happened?'

'Way, way too much, Dan.'

She runs sobbing and retching to the bathroom. Sitting on the cold white tiles her head is spinning, reeling, too much to feel. All the words never said. She bangs her forehead hard on the toilet bowl. From what seems a million miles away she hears the front door bell. Sighing, she pulls herself up from the floor, tears running down her face. Pads down the hallway through the trash heap she has made, and opens the door. It could only be one person.

'Hi, Bernadette.' Falls, sobbing into her arms.

For once, no recriminations, no telling off. Just her friend's welcome arms of acceptance.

'Oh, Jen. Jen, Darling. We just never know do we?' She goes to the kitchen looking under the sink for a brush and pan to sweep up all the mess.

Days go by, then weeks and months. Bob's death has left a space but more like a recovery from a long disease. A time to exhale. She and Dan laugh together again and watch episodes of Homicide and The Sullivans, scrunched up on the old brown lounge together, just like the old days.

She gets rid of the old velvet lounge, the Namco setting in the kitchen, even the fridge. All replaced with something she and Dan pick out together. She works like a mad woman, pulling down all the curtains and blinds, dragging the wallpaper off the walls and painting them, staying up all night until it is done, trying to remove every vestige of memory of Bob from their living space.

Walking down the side passage outside, she comes upon the trashed Noritake, still scrunched up in newspaper next to the garbage bin. She carefully takes it out, piece by piece and brings it inside.

At two in the morning, she falls onto the unmade bed and sleeps.

Jenny had returned to work two days after the funeral. It was after getting the second dosage of medication for a patient hopelessly wrong that she realised it was time to take a break from work.

She sat with Caroline at their usual coffee spot. 'It's really weird though, I just feel nothing. Nothing at all. I'm so exhausted 'cos of no sleep but I just feel completely numb. Is that normal?'

Caroline leaned back on the lounge chair and forked another piece of chocolate cake into her mouth.

'Look, everyone grieves in a different way. It'll hit you soon enough. Start writing again in your journal. Plus, maybe you need to see a counsellor to help you and Danny through this?'

'Yeah. Maybe. And why do I feel so guilty all of a sudden? I did all I could.'

'Jen, darling. You certainly went the extra hundred miles with that husband of yours. He is gone. Try a find a few happy memories in the mix and go with that.'

Jen looked dazed and blank. 'The thing is, Darl, I just don't know who I am now.'

CHAPTER 26

Richard ran like a man being chased. Thudding across the wet sand in the dusk light heading into the pursuing dark. No Sweet Caroline now. Just escape. With Marilyn in the hospice now he knew time was running out and there was no escaping the fact that he was about to be alone. Very alone. The news about her baby has hit him hard.

'I'm not angry about the baby. Just, just why didn't you tell me before? That's all. I would've tried to help you find her, Mazzie.'

He was running even before he reached the wide open space of the beach.

On the beach now, squelching in the deepening, wet sucking sand and slowed by it, he let the tears come, great gulping sobs that stopped him in his tracks as he bent over to catch his breath. 'I've run out ... I've run out.' He repeated it over and over until finally, sitting in the shallows as the relentless tide came in deeper and deeper, he lay back, salt water rushing into his ears and hair, surrendering to it somehow and to all that the fractions of his life had cancelled down to.

The beach was like his wailing wall, his place of petition to a God who seemed a long way off. Sorry for his failures, his inadequacies, things said. And not said. And now, a daughter she might never meet.

Jenny sat quietly beside the woman she has come to know well, the soft hiss of oxygen filling the darkened room. Now and then Marilyn opens her eyes and, finding Jenny's face lapses back to her peace-filled space. It had been a moment of great clarity the day before when, as Jenny popped in and out to check on her, she suddenly roused and propped up on one elbow. Marilyn struggled to form the words but as she held Jenny's eyes she whispered, 'Richard ... Richard...'

Jenny was immediately on her feet. 'Do you want me to get him for you?'

She shook her head. Jenny watched the opiates kicking in as her eyes rolled back.

Suddenly she is awake, clutching at the air. 'He has a lot to tell you ... a lot.'

She falls back on the pillows and sleeps.

In the subtly lit corridor, death flits in shadows in and out of rooms. Outside the door Jenny hears footsteps approaching. Richard enters quietly going straight to the bed. Sand spills from his upturned jeans cuffs. His shirt back is wet and sandy. 'She said anything?'

Jenny shakes her head and leaves the room. Was that just the drugs or did she really mean...?

What could Richard possibly have of interest to tell her? What does Marilyn even know about them? Is there even a them?

Shaking her head she checks the time. She re-enters the room and gives Marilyn's hand a gentle squeeze.

'See you tomorrow. You sleep now.'

With her shift finished and the handover given to the next RN on duty, she runs to the car and starts the drive home. The late afternoon light is still dazzling after the subdued hospice lights.

Out along Bunjip Bay Road, the Ti Tree lake is silent and black now.

A flock of white egrets flutters from the reeds into a very blue sky. She parks under the old cream-peeling Ti trees and thinks of Marilyn, dying in a room in a Hospice.

An unfinished life with a man who will never understand her. She wishes she had known Marilyn in her earlier life. Bob had never encouraged them to get together. In a small town like Bunjip, everyone knows everyone. Not many secrets here. She thinks of Danny, now without a Dad. Looks at her own life, spanning away like a great unfurled sheet flapping into nowhere. Rests her head on her arms on the steering wheel and lets the tears come. So many words left unsaid between her and Bob.

Last night Danny had come in to her bedroom before he went off to his room. Sat on the edge of her bed while she brushed her hair. Without a word, he took the brush from her and began the long strokes in her fair hair, watching the sparks lifting the hair up.

'Mum. Can I ask you something?'

'Always.'

'Dad had a big heart attack, didn't he? I was just wondering if, if it hurt or anything?'

Jenny let her breath out in little jidders. She could see his little trusting face in the mirror.

'No, Darl. No, he would have gone quickly, I'm sure.'

Danny dropped the brush on the bed and snuggled in his mother's arms, butting his face in her neck and shoulder.

'I don't miss him, Mum. I'm glad...'

Jenny rocked him in her arms. 'Shhhh now. I know. I know.' They were great gulping sobs that shook his body. Jenny held him tight until he settled.

'We'll be Okay, Danny. We'll be fine, you and me.'

She drives into the old tree-bordered driveway. She is home in a way she never thought possible. Finally, a peaceful house, decorated the way she always wanted. The new white curtains blow in a gust of wind through the open front window. Danny lies on the lounge, telly on and an opened packet of Peak Frean biscuits and a Milo on the coffee table. She stands in the hallway listening to normal. To quiet and to peace.

'Hey you.' She ruffles his hair, now almost shoulder length. He looks up smiling through a mouthful of biscuits with a milk moustache surrounding.

The garden beckons after a long day sitting with Marilyn. Making a cup of tea she muses again on Marilyn's last words to her. They might well be the last words she hears from her now.

Most of the town turned out for Marilyn Bonsall's funeral. Her Aunty Norma had come back up from Sydney and helped Richard organise the catering for those who wanted to come back after the funeral. Lots of people remembered her from years ago. The house filled to capacity, with people spreading onto the wide veranda.

Jenny sees Richard at the heavily laden dining table. She is looking into the eyes of a lost boy. She goes out to the veranda and pats the old Labrador who thumps his tail in gratitude. She sits on the edge of the Lazy-boy where Marilyn spent her last months in the shade of the Bougainvillea, now a wall of bright red blossom.

Glancing down she sees a brown envelope with Confidential emblazoned across the back and the Government emblem. She picks it up ready to give it to Richard. She can hear him in the lounge room agreeing with someone. She walks in holding the envelope out and passes it to him with a smile. He jumps back as if shot, grabbing the envelope with both hands, excusing himself from the man he is with.

'We need to talk. And soon.' He puts his arm round her shoulders. She shrugs out of his hold and moves back to the veranda, Richard following.

'Now is not the time, whatever it is.'

'No. OK. I'll call by sometime. Is that OK?'

Jenny shrugs and makes her way back into the lounge full of people, ready to make her excuses to go.

CHAPTER 27

It's six weeks since Marilyn died.

Jenny is in the kitchen cleaning up last night's dishes and pans.

Danny, board under his arm, heads towards the front door.

'Mu-um. Someone at the door.'

She wipes her wet sudsy hands on a tea towel and tightens the cord of her pyjama pants.

'OK, well answer it then.'

As he opens the door Danny sees a tall lean man with dark curly hair and steady brown eyes.

'Hi.'

'You must be Danny. Gee, you're a lot like your Mum, hey?'

Unsure, Danny turns away and Jenny is right behind him. She is smiling that tight smile that says she is on her back foot.

'Richard. Yes, this is Danny. Come on in.'

Danny mumbles a hello and is starts for the door. He glances at the stranger in his house and gives a half-smile. 'Back soon Mum. Surf's up today.'

The board's on the bike rack in no time.

Richard and Jenny eye each other steadily. She puts the kitchen bench between them. Feels as awkward as a teenage school girl. Hand a bit trembly so she pops it behind her. She can feel the current between them and fears to speak in case it stops.

'Cuppa? We can go out into the garden. Nice out there today.'

Say My Name

She carries the tray out and they sit under the Lilli-Pilli, a bunch of noisy Miners cheeping and scattering pink berries all around them like confetti.

'Look,' says Richard, 'I know its early days and all that but I was just wondering, well, there's a fund raiser for that family that lost their son. You know, got taken by a shark?'

Jenny looks up from her tea, looks into very blue steady eyes. Feels the pull of the tide there. Lets the tide take her where it will.

She smiles a wide relaxed face changer. 'Yes. That'd be nice. Look. It's a small town, shall I meet you there?'

His is a slow smile. It's a crinkle-at-the-eyes smile and draws her in. Flustered, she looks away. Feels her heart race a little. Looks back. He's relaxed, leaning back in the chair, legs out. Like he belongs in this garden, on these chairs. She smiles back.

'Naah. How about I pick you up. Seven OK?' He stands up and stretches, then takes a brown envelope out of his pocket.

'Want to talk about this sometime soon, too.'

Jenny recognises it as the envelope from under Marilyn's veranda lounge.

'Yep. OK. Gotta get ready for work now. I'll walk you out.'

Stands in the front doorway, waving. The same doorway she has fled through so many times. Her shoulders give an involuntary twitch at the memory. Relaxes in the safety of the quiet calm house and lets fear fly away like an old crow whooshed off a perch. Takes a deep breath. Lets it go. Turning, she walks into the back garden, rose bushes blooming now and bees in everything. She dares to enjoy life without Bob and feels the Fruit-Tingle bubbling at her edges.

The fundraiser is a predictable small town deal. Everyone is so sad for the Jensons who have lost their fifteen-year-old son, Rod. The two younger sons stand around, not quite knowing where to put themselves. Jenny can hear snatched conversations about The Seven Mile and its dangerous reefs and the shark problem but it won't bring the young lad back.

She thinks about the finality of death and all the words that can never now be said. Thinks about the words she would've liked to have said to Bob. Or maybe she couldn't have? As Caroline had said a few years ago, you don't know anyone 'til you live with them. How true. But grateful, so grateful for Danny boy. A little girl would've been lovely as well but ... wasn't to be.

A three-piece band is doing its best to cheer everyone up with some Top 40s stuff, but every song seems tinged with sadness. There is a heaviness over the crowd, despite raffles, lucky door prizes. Richard is surrounded with people who want to talk about Marilyn and bring consolation to him. He is used to always being the centre of attention. Available now too, in a way. He glances over frequently to Jenny, sipping her drink, watching the crowd. It was obvious that this was not going to be a workable night for them. She leaves quietly and unnoticed, throwing him a smile and a half wave.

The next day is a Sunday. Richard appears on the doorstep by nine, knocking for entry, waving the Sunday paper. They drink tea under the Lilli-Pilli again, and he and Danny kick a ball around the garden a bit. The bees buzz in the Salvia and the great swathe of deep orange Nasturtiums. Rosellas shriek to each other, flitting rainbows across the garden.

Richard sits down puffing from all the running about and picks up the Sunday paper, scanning the headlines.

'What part of the paper do you want, Jen? Travel? Books?'

'Yep. All of that.' She reaches out her hand and takes a section. They sit in companionable silence, drinking tea and reading, as if it's been that way for twenty years.

Jenny smiles at the scene, relaxing back into the recliner, gazing into middle distance.

CHAPTER 28

It's a Tuesday morning in September. Jenny is in the garden weeding on her hands and knees when she hears the vroom and splutter of the postie bike as it disappears around the corner, shaking the Jasmine vine, shuddering off fragrance. Jenny walks slowly down to the mailbox. Her birthday is the next day, and she expects a few cards this year. It's the big one. Forty years old. Hard to believe. First birthday since Bob drowned. Celebration this time. She grabs out two cards, one from her sister in Perth and the other she doesn't recognise. She turns it over. No address on the back.

As soon as she sees the spidery crawl, she knows. Her eyes race to the end of the message. Her hand flies to her mouth as she draws breath in quickly. Something deep inside her thuds and changes course quickly.

'It's Mum.' Her heart leaps in her chest, as longing and rage fight a duel. Her fingers are shaking as she opens the pink envelope. She had done her best to edit her mother out of her life's text. And now, here it was.

"Dear Jennifer, I know it has been a long time and for that I am truly sorry. I know your birthday is coming. I wouldn't blame you if you want nothing to do with me as what I did is unforgivable. I have never stopped loving you and your sister and I think of you every day. Could we meet do you think? Here is my Post Office address." At the bottom of the message was a Post Office address in a town not too far away. Knowing she was so close set off alarm bells and sirens.

As well as the whisper of hope.

With a shock, Jenny sits down hard on the log near her parked car. Looking again at the letter and re-reading it and its implications, she gets up quickly, placing the letter back into the envelope and pocketing it in her jeans. She runs into the house for the car keys, leaving the house unlocked, the front door whining back on its hinges.

Bernadette's? No, she'll want to forgive and forget straight away. Won't be doing that. Caroline? More balanced but at work right now. Richard, maybe? No, he has his own stuff to deal with. He was probably at work plastering at The Bay.

She heads straight to the Seven Mile. Calming down, she concentrates on the road and the small amounts of traffic going to the beach. The day is clear and sunny, the sky cloudless and still. Too early for swimming, only just out of winter. Even as a kid, Jenny had never had an obsessive urge to dive into the water no matter what the season as some of the kids did.

Her own drama seems in total contrast to the unfolding day all around her. She passes the Ti Tree lake, now sombre and dark but cheered up with a few splashy kids at the edge, squealing together. Finally in the car park, she reefs the keys out and slams the door. Her heart is thudding fast. She puts her hands on her knees, 'Slow down girl. Slow down.'

Finding a dune, she slumps amongst the silver-grey grass, wriggling and rounding the sand into her body contours. Time for a long, intentional think. Disengaged somehow, from the fact that her mother after all these years, 30 to be exact, has now decided to make contact. Well. That's some birthday present. Something she has longed for all her life. And now it is right here, right now.

CHAPTER 29

The smartly dressed woman, heels clacking down the lino hallway, wafts musky perfume like a smokescreen around her. She struggles with a heavy suitcase, which pulls one shoulder down to the left. Quick as a flash a door opens in the hallway and a wizened face with a bald head calls out, 'Moving out are you, Love? Don't forget the rent you owe me.' And slams the door hard. He knows it won't happen.

With a sniff Hermione Slade keeps walking. Nose in the air she ignores the open doors on either side of the hallway, horse races blaring from radios. Ignores old Reg, leering round the doorway at her.

'Struth! Look at this. Leavin' us are ya? Nose so high if it rained you'd drown.' A laugh like a rusty key rasping in a lock.

Seen better days, summed up Hermione Slade. Down the twelve stairs, clump ... clump with the suitcase, turns left into the busy city street with its sudden assault of clatter and honking horns. She doesn't look back. Ducks into the first café open and drops exhausted into a seat at the back. The waitress who serves her is young and sullen. One eye has a fading bruise at the corner and she does her best not to stare at it.

God what a mess. On my own, no husband and lost my girls. She sucks her top lip with her teeth, and tries to collect herself as the edges of memories threaten to drag her out into the deep. She shakes herself free of emotion as the waitress dumps the teapot and cup down hard, staring at her as one soul recognising another. Hermione pours the tea. No regrets, remember?

In the Newsagent she looks for a birthday card. Not too soppy, not too plain. Imagine that. Her eldest girl now forty. Bet she won't want to see me but anyway, here goes. She finds a clear bit of space near the counter, borrows a pen and begins to write.

Nothing to lose. She gives a hard laugh. Lost it all, anyway. Derek's gone too.

Remembers the day when the world stopped. Well, began in another way too. For a while anyway. Bill Larkins, "Larkey," they called him. Tall, charming with a great sense of humour and a way of listening to her that made her feel alive. Everything Derek wasn't. He had finally lured her off with his promises of excitement and travel. Away from the boring country town where she logged off her days in a stuporous fog with Derek and the kids, all needing what was left of her.   Bill called on all the women in the neighbourhood with his van full of pretty dresses and handbags, bringing the world to them, trapped as they were with no transport except one irregular bus a day. And he was a reader too. That was what talked her into letting him in. First the kitchen then the lounge. Finally, there was no turning back and they were booking hotel rooms after that. An easy conquest. Bored housewife plus inattentive husband. Bound to happen.

They had run off to Sydney one Saturday morning. Said he had plenty of contacts, plenty of work. What was she thinking? She'd already started not coming home and had completely forgotten the afternoon of the ballet. Remembered it now with such a loathing and disgust of herself. She and Bill had gone to shows, to plays. The money ran out eventually and it had only been a matter of a few years before Bill was casting his eye and actually the rest of his body, over the assorted crowd at the local pub. It had ended for them predictably when a younger more exciting version had crossed his line of vision.

Finding herself alone again, Hermione had swallowed her pride and got work as a waitress. Anywhere and everywhere. Got her hair cut in a sort of Audrey Hepburn coconut cut, which framed her slightly aristocratic face with its archy nose and deep brown eyes. But after a while, there seemed to be far too many pointless dinner dates with no substance attached.

She heard about Derek's passing through someone she ran slap bang into in George Street in the city, from up home. Another huge ladle of guilt to swallow. Those were the dark days, when truth hit like a meteor, unexpectedly in the early hours of morning before dawn, as it does. Quite recently, she had landed a job in a down-at-heel boarding house in the Paddington back streets just at the right time. Or the wrong time, as it turned out. With nowhere to stay that night and no job she realised beggars can't be choosers.

The old bald-headed coot who managed the place offered her a room and board if she'd do the cooking and cleaning. He held out a dry leathery hand and cleared his throat noisily. 'Call me Ronnie,' he had said. He looked at her like a butcher about to section out a side of beef. And with as much hunger.

Reluctantly she had agreed to the deal. Life was etched on her face now and the future, if there was one, seemed very bleak. Felt the grey cloud heavy on her mind, moving in again. That old familiar dark bird of hopelessness spread its wings out over her, hovering, looking to land, rendering her immobile. It was a hard slog, the guesthouse. She was no spring chicken anymore and every bone and joint agreed. Humping the vacuum cleaner up several flights of stairs each day was taking its toll. The kitchen was dank and full of eons of cooking smells embedded in the greasy unwashed walls. She cooked the basics: chops and three veg, greasy oxtail soup, stewing steak and shepherd's pie. Most of the guests were down on their luck and barely engaged with each other beyond passing the salt. Heads down, eyes averted. Hook in.

Two women with bloodshot eyes and noses to match, sat without conversation at a table off to the back of the dining room. Somehow the women seemed more pathetic to have landed here at Ronnie's place. Like the Last Resort Hotel. The walls were dirty cream, plastic flowers in a cracked amber vase was the only decoration. An empty square where once a painting had hung told the story. Apathy and loss hung in the air speaking its own language.

Everything ached in Hermione's body. The varicose veins in the back of her legs stood out like a map of her life. Washing up that night, with the help of one of the women from the back table who felt sorry for her, she knew it was all too much. The vacuum cleaner seemed heavier than usual with its long hose and short cord, particularly on the third floor landing.

Exhausted, she dropped onto her bed, desperate for rest. Tears of regret ran like a stream looking for home. She knew it was enough. A plan began to form. As daylight snaked under the thin, white terylene curtain in her bedroom she knew what she had to do. Packing her one suitcase, she dressed quickly. With one last look around, she left the room for the last time. She'd forgotten how many weeks' rent was owing. She could hear the other residents stirring in their rooms, like the scuttling of rats. The dawn light over the city was cold and dirty. Mist filled the pockets between the buildings, grey and austere in the early gloom. The shop windows were dimly lit and full of naked static models waiting to be clothed by the window dresser. Without genitals and facial expression, they lacked identity.

She frowned at the comparison to her own life, and crossed the empty road to the bus station. A sudden gust of gritty wind sent the top pages of the morning papers outside the newsagents hurtling down the grey pavement.

The city had shut its door to her now. She began to long for windswept beaches and the sound of seagulls. She found the Greyhound Office and booked her ticket. The mournful moan of a departing train blasted the still space of a new morning.

She sat down in the waiting room, the smell of yesterday's smokers thick in the windowless room. Hermione rummaged about in her handbag and fished out a crumpled packet of Craven A and lit up, inhaling the welcome smoke and grateful for the filter tip. A large woman as crumpled as an unmade bed sat down next to her. She leaned into her with a sly but desperate look. 'Give us a fag love, will ya?' Hermione passed her the pack and matches without engaging. The woman was off out the door, taking the cigarettes and matches with her. Hermione heard her thudding feet as she ran off down the street. She stubbed out the fag to save for later. 'Damn. It'll be a long time between smokes.'

The bus heading out of Sydney was crowded and cramped. She found herself wedged beside an obese woman who talked loudly and endlessly about her marvellous children and even more marvellous grand-children, producing photos of all out of a grubby envelope, for evidence. Hermione feigned sleep and finally switched her off. The woman then opened her packet of Minties, rattling around half the night and throwing lolly wrappers on the floor. It was going to be a long trip.

She'd managed to find Jenny's address in the Electoral Roll as it turned out. The bus rounded the corner coming into Coffs Harbour, the sunset bathing everything in a rosy light. Still a few hours to go but a hot pie was a welcome respite at the Service station on the outskirts of town. The bus trundled through the night, rarely stopping. Sleep evaded her and she resigned herself to wakefulness.

As the bus pulled into Bunjip, Hermione straightened up and readied herself for whatever lay ahead. Steeled herself from face to foot. She dragged her suitcase along to the beach-front, where cafés were just starting to open up and put their tables and umbrellas out the front. She felt the stares of people as she stood on the edge of the dunes in her city clothes and heels, suitcase beside her. She'd have to take her chances on a welcome from Jenny. Exhausted from no sleep and a long journey she walked up Beach Street to the first guest house she saw. A woman with a bland face and no particular expression, a tight blonde perm and too much blue eye shadow presided at the front desk.

'Just the one night, is it?' she asked Hermione. 'This time of year you can have three nights for the price of two. Yeah?'

'Yes. That's lovely thank you. Three nights will work.'

'You look done in, love. Room 5. Top of the stairs.'

Hermione looked up at the flight of stairs with dread, knowing how heavy her suitcase was, then back at the permed woman, hoping for a break.

The woman's glance was steady and knowing. 'Oh alright. Maybe Room 3. Just along the corridor here.'

Hermione took the key on its large wooden holder, thankful for small mercies.

She fell onto the bed, fully clothed and into a dreamless sleep.

Light rain spattered on the window waking her up. Squally clouds promising more ganged up low in the sky. She sat up on the edge of the bed, heavy with the realisation of the thirty-year gap in Jenny's life. They no longer knew each other.

She padded across the cold tiles of the bathroom. Nothing ventured, nothing gained. Feeling suddenly nauseated she vomited into the toilet bowl. She washed her face then fell back onto the bed.

Later in the morning Hermione stood at the doorway of the guest house wishing she had an umbrella. She'd done her make up carefully. Not too much, not too bright. Picked out the floral dress that never let her down. So far, anyway. With a determined sigh, she pulled her shoulders back and began the slow walk through the beach town, fluttering with red and white striped awnings.

She checked her street map every now and again and as the number of shops dwindled down to nothing, she noticed she was in Bunjip Bay suburbia. Timber clad cottages and newer brick houses lined the streets. Tidy gardens and fences everywhere. She began to take notice of the street names. Forty-three Jacaranda Avenue. Third on the left. Passed Hibiscus Avenue, then Poinciana. Here it is. Jacaranda Avenue. She turned into the street, her heart pounding.

Hesitated at number forty-one, the house before number 43, heart pounding in her ears, gathering herself together.

Looking from the street, she could see a timber house set well back from the road. A long gravel driveway bordered by Jacarandas and Poincianas curved towards it. Hermione took a deep breath and began the walk towards the front door, every scrunch giving away her presence. A blue Holden was parked under a Jacaranda and a ginger cat rolled over in the sun and blinked at her. The ground was strewn in mauve bells from the Jaca, cascading down in every light breeze. With shaking hands she rang the bell next to the front door. Heard it echo into the hollow space of the hallway. Then she heard a scurry of footsteps behind the door which squeaked back on its hinges.

Hermione is on her back foot. She knows it. Jenny knows it. They stand looking at each other steadily for what seems like forever. Gazing down the years. Jenny is pale. Composed. One word sums up her mother: Ravaged. Her once wavy chestnut hair is now well speckled with grey and could do with a good trim. The lines around her mouth have set like hardened concrete. There is a tremor to her lips but it could be nerves. There is still an elegance, but almost hidden by years of hard yards.

Hermione gives a tentative smile and flutters out a hand. Jenny flinches as though stung.

'May I, may I ?' and stumbles on the step.

Jenny spins around. 'Come in. I'll make some tea.' She walks down the hallway, her whole body is tight and shaking. It's been too long. Way too long. Hermione stands in the pinewood kitchen, a total stranger. Her daughter's house. Finally. Jenny stands at the window, her back to her mother, her hands trembling.

'Tea? Or coffee? I wouldn't know anymore.' Jenny feels the anger rising like mercury.

'Tea. Tea's fine. Milk and none.' She half perches on the pine stool up at the bench.

'I'm sorry Jen, but...'

'Not now. Later.'

She gets some Jatz from the cupboard and cheese from the fridge. Hermione watches the glint of the knife. Chop. Chop. Chop.

Jenny, still chopping asks, 'So. All these years. And why now?'

Her mother sighs and looks away. Darts a glance at Jenny's closed face. They are two cats circling.

'Look, it didn't work out. It was tricky. Too much to tell.' Her voice faded away as she gazed through the kitchen window from her perch on the stool.

Jenny stops chopping, willing herself into the present moment. The silence is an empty grave of held breath.

'Try me.' She puts her hands on her hips. Willing her mother to look at her face.

The chasm hangs between them in the uncovered space. A mower starts up in next door's garden and they both jump as if shot. Nothing moves in the room. In a shaft of sunlight dust dances. A moment they had both longed for, ebbing and flowing.

Jenny takes a long look at her mother. She is like a smaller shrunken version of the mother she remembered. Vulnerable, even. Feels the shaken cocktail of rage and loss well up in its acid bath to

156

her gullet. Grabs for the glass of water on the sink to swallow it down quickly. She turns her back on Hermione.

'Nothing. No word. No letter. All these years, Mum. And you waltz in like nothing's happened.' She bangs the glass down on the bench. Thank God Daniel isn't here.

Hermione can't look at her daughter. She slides off the stool and collects her handbag.

'Look, I shouldn't have come. I'll leave this to another time.'

'No. We are here now. We need to talk.'

As Jenny spins around to get the kettle, she knocks the glass sugar bowl with her wrist. It crashes to the floor in a mess of glass and white sugar. Both women gasp.

Jenny is on her knees in a flash, grabbing for the brush and pan in the cupboard. 'Damn. Damn and blast.' They pick up the pieces together, Hermione scrabbling about on the floor in her best floral dress, saying nothing, grateful for the moment. Jenny sweeps like a mad woman then sits back on her heels. They are both sitting on the floor. She allows her mother's thin arms to wrap around her and cradle her once again as an underground river flows through them both. She strokes Jenny's long hair as she sobs into her mother's bony shoulder. Notices a glass shard has cut her index finger and ignores it.

'I'm so sorry, Jen. So, so sorry. I don't know if you can ever...' Her voice trails off.

Jenny shakes herself free of the embrace and blows her nose.

'Look, Mum. I've got a son who knows nothing about you. He'll be home soon. Can we do this another time?'

Hermione scans the fridge door loaded with its display of photos and notes. Right in the middle is a photo of a blond-haired, blue-eyed teenager looking shyly at the lens. A smattering of freckles sprinkle across his nose.

'Is that your boy? Is that Danny? Someone told me...' Her voice is almost reverent. 'He's got your father's eyes. Your colouring though. What is his father like?'

Jenny's face closes. 'Was. Bob's gone. Drowned a while ago now. He was ... he was dark. You know, I mean hair and eyes and that.'

Hermione nods and stands up. Brushes her dress into order.

'God. So much to catch up on.' Her eyes light up. 'I've got a grandson?' She smiles and her whole face softens. Jenny stays statue cold.

'Where are you staying? I can give you a lift if you like on the way to the school?'

'I'm at Seabreeze Guest house near the front there. I, I don't drink anymore. Bit of a liver thing now. Could I, could I ring you? I know the number. I looked it up.'

Without waiting for an answer she turns and walks down the hallway to the front door. She doesn't look back. She opens the door, shutting it quietly behind her.

Jenny runs down the hallway yanking open the door. 'Mum. I do want to see you, OK?'

Her mother turns and nods. 'I'll be back soon. Maybe at the weekend if that's OK?'

Jenny nods, tears streaming down her face. She leans back on the closed door and shudders.

CHAPTER 30

Saturday in Bunjip Bay. Sun splashes along the beach-front awnings, and like a stage play, cafés spring to life and the weekend traffic begins its run. Hermione has ditched her city clothes and looks like one of the crowd. Almost. She has even managed to land a desk job in the local real estate when she went in enquiring about a cheap rental. Things were looking up. A few pegs higher than the Sydney guest house, that's for sure.

Things have changed in the beach culture that she remembered from thirty years ago. Derek would occasionally drive the family down from Gideon Vale for a walk on the beach and an ice cream but it had never been part of family life.

Mobs of blond-headed surfies all hypnotised by waves and water, gazed out to sea like lost mariners blinkered against the rest of the world. The lure of the sea was as ancient and primal as the search for home, calling like a siren to come out deeper.

A new Health Food shop, cinema still here, couple of dress shops now. Bunjip Bay had changed but so had she. Shame cloaks her every move and thought, impaling her on its rusty hook. It meets her in every face, imagined with every look, solemn or benign. Her card to Fiona had been sent just that morning. A long letter of regret and contrition, journeying all the way to Perth. Eight years old when her mother had left, she now lives as a successful journalist on a Perth

159

newspaper. Still single and with no desire to be any other way. As far away as possible from the East Coast and plans to stay there.

The flat Hermione was shown was damp and mildewed with a musty dank smell. It is affordable though and with a coat of paint and some air Hermione feels she could cope and cope well. It's the downstairs flat of four. Two up, two down. Bright red hibiscus bushes fill the bare patched lawn in front which badly needs a good mow. An old vinyl mustard-coloured sofa slumps in the lounge room, sagging from the weight of too many bodies. The kitchen is clean enough and has a fridge and stove. She opens the kitchen windows and breathes in sea air. Sits down on the old lounge and feels the pain of loss but the hope of some sort of restoration.

This'll do. And I have a job. Can't be all bad. Things are looking up.

CHAPTER 31

'What? Thirty years? You're kidding, right?' Richard holds his hands out as if ready to catch a giant ball.

'I wish I was. Such a bolt from the blue.'

'So ... what's that like then? Must be so weird.'

Jenny curls one leg underneath her on the lounge.

'Yeah. Dunno. I sort of grew up with no Mum but always wanted her to come back. And now she's back and I'm not sure what I feel. Pretty angry to be honest. We've all missed out on so much. Maybe too much. She left us when we needed her most. Dad was just devastated. He never really recovered. Did his best though. For us, I mean. Fiona and me.'

'So, what happened to your Dad? He's not around now is he?'

'Dad? Just sort of faded away. We never really knew to be honest. Just found him dead in his bed one morning.'

'And your sister? Fiona? Where's she in all this?' Richard glances over at her. 'Sorry Darl. I'm interrogating you. This can wait.'

Jenny is far away in memory, looking into middle distance. 'I'd met Bob by then. We just kind of got on with it. The rest is history, as they say.'

Richard reaches out and touches her leg and leaves his hand there. This time she didn't flinch. He looks right into her eyes. 'Must be hard for you, this.'

Relaxing into his gaze she feels the comfort and lets her head fall onto his shoulder.

'You have something you wanted to show me though, don't you?'

'Look, not now. It can wait 'til another time.'

This man feels safe. Feels warm. Comfortable, even.

Richard pulls away first. 'A walk on the beach?'

'It's a bit windy. But, well ok.'

Sand blows against their bare legs with a sting. The crazy star grass billows about their heads and makes walking nearly impossible. He grabs her hand

'C'mon lets run.'

They run like children along the windswept beach, holding hands, faces to the sky. Jenny falls into the sand laughing and Richard follows, his face against hers. It was a long slow gentle kiss, followed by another. Jenny pulled away first and lies against his shoulder, slightly out of breath. They smile into each other's eyes, letting love surface from some deep place in them both.

'Well then.' Jenny's blue eyes are dancing.

They begin the walk back along the beach, arm in arm, bodies touching.

Richard stops suddenly and points up the beach.

'There's our sand dune. Where we met for the first time. That's pretty different hey?'

Jenny puts her arm around his waist, pulling him in close. 'Wait 'til you meet the real "sweet Caroline" mister.'

CHAPTER 32

The pain arrived silently and unexpectedly like a stranger waiting in the shadows. Hermione woke from a deep place with a groan as sharp pain bit into her right side. She looked through a blur at the bedside clock. Three a.m. The pain hit again and again, causing her to lurch from her warm bed and walk around the flat. She held her side, rigid and gasping for breath. Fumbled in the bathroom for the headache pills, and in her rush, spilled them all over the floor. Exhaling and gripping the bathroom sink she gazed unblinking into the mirror. A thin pale face met her gaze, sallow and hunted.

Later that morning she sat in Dr. Brewer's surgery. He was a dour little Scot, his face closed like a sphincter and never a smile to be had. Well recommended though and very thorough. She stretched out on the cold sheet and let him prod and poke her stomach. She cried out with pain when he pressed her right side.

'Let's just do a few tests first, shall we? Then we will know for sure what's going on.'

He kept writing without looking up.

'That's it then, is it?' asked Hermione

'That's it. Yes.'

She got up and left the surgery, a swathe of papers in her hand, and walked down to the beachfront and along towards the Estuary wall. She found the relentless slap-slap of the water against the long stone walls calming but the numb of shock still sat festering, emitting the tiniest bubbles of reality to the surface. Her life in the balance. Again. Looking at the pathology requests she saw the sardonic face of fear staring her down, grinding her guts.

With a deep sigh she got up and walked towards the hospital, looking for the pathology department and whatever lay ahead.

Caroline tucked her legs underneath her on the old brown leather lounge at the very back wall of their café, stirring her tea. Jenny sat tense in the opposite chair, holding a steaming cup in her hands, frowning into the distance.

'So ... you're really falling for Richard aren't you?'

Jenny gave a smile that lit up her eyes. 'He's nice. He's safe. And he and Danny get on pretty good too.'

'So, what's the problem then?'

Jenny fought back the tears and put her cup down on the coffee table with deliberation. She put her head in her hands.

'It's just ... it's just that...'

'What? What? Finally you get a chance to be happy with a nice guy and...?' she trailed off, splaying her hands in question.

'Well, I just think it'll be only a matter of time before he, well, loses interest.'

'Don't be mad, Jen. You're a fabulous catch for any man. You're caring and kind.'

'Look Darl, it's the story of my life. Everybody leaves. My Mum leaves, not just for a short time but thirty years Caroline! I obviously didn't have what Bob needed and now and now... even Danny doesn't want to be around me much anymore so...' She began to cry hard. Caroline came over and hugged her, patting her back.

'Jenny, Jenny, Jenny. Danny is just being a teenager. That's just normal stuff. Take it from me. I've raised two of them. Lucky to get more than a grunt from boys at this age. Bob didn't even half deserve you and wore down any self-confidence you might have brought into the marriage. And your mother, well, that's just the most selfish thing any mother could do. Can you imagine leaving Danny? No, of course not.'

Jenny relaxed into Caroline's arms and let out a shaky breath. She fumbled for her hanky and blew her nose hard.

'Thanks Caroline. What would I do without a friend like you?'

'Here. Finish your tea.. All I can say is Richard had better be as good as he's cracked up to be. Or else.' She made a sign like a slit throat, and smiled.

Jenny gulped down her tea and checked her watch. With a gasp she was up and at the door.

'Gotta go, Darl. Got a shift this afternoon.'

She turned as she opened the door of the café.

'Thanks Caroline. I mean it.'

She hurried home and dressed in her uniform quickly. When she got to the Oncology Ward and walked into the staff room one of the other nurses, Terri, looked at her with a frown.

'What are you doing here? We swapped shifts, remember? You're doing mine next Wednesday.'

'Oh. Clean forgot. Yes, of course I remember now. Whoo hoo. Day off. See ya.'

And she was gone.

She sat behind the old Holden steering wheel, wondering what to do. Found herself driving to the Seven Mile. Like the car knew its own way there now.

The breeze was strong today in a cloudless blue sky. Just a few on the beach mid-week. She stripped off her shoes and stockings and got out of the car. Looked around the sand hills before stepping onto the warm silky sand. Felt the warmth between her toes.

She took in the whole beach. Couples, a few girls getting an early suntan for summer, a couple of dog walkers. She glanced up fondly towards the sand hills, so different in broad daylight. Her space. Her private place.

There was only one couple up there today. The woman was suntanned and in a black bikini, throwing her head back laughing. The man she was with was slim and suntanned. She squinted against the sun, recognising something familiar. Or rather someone familiar. With a start, she realised it was Richard. The woman beside him, laughing, was Caroline. Her whole body went cold and heavy. An immobility rooted her to the spot. She turned back to the car and like a robot, drove home. A sadness like no other, from somewhere very deep washed over her like an unexpected wave in the shallows.

She waited a week. A very long week. Finally, with a heavy heart she called in on Caroline. She had managed to put Richard off all week but he was beginning to wonder what was up. He was still on about something important he wanted to share with her too.

'Well, it can just wait now. I knew it was too good to be true. Men. All the same. Just a matter of time.'

Caroline answered the door with a smile. She took a step back and frowned at Jenny.

'Dear God, what's happened now? You'd better come in love.'

Jenny sat with her arms folded over her chest, everything coiled, looking at the floor, not daring to look at Caroline. Sadness and anger coupled and raged.

'What? What is it?'

Angry now, Jenny blurted, 'I told you it was only a matter of time. But you were the last person...' she burst into tears. Caroline looked bewildered.

'Hang on. What are you talking...'

'You know. On the beach last Wednesday. I saw you. With Richard. You looked pretty cosy, you two.'

Caroline threw back her head and laughed. 'You must be joking. We just happened to be on the beach at the same time. We were actually both raving about you, if you must know. He is very keen. On you, I mean.'

Jenny looked up at Caroline nodding and smiling at her.

'What? Really? Oh. Looks like I got the wrong impression. I hope.'

'Come here, you. He's crazy about you. Don't be mad. He's not my type anyway,' she said with a smile and pulled Jenny in for a hug.

CHAPTER 33

Hermione sat looking out at the red hibiscus blooming outside her window. Too much to process. She grabbed her purse and slammed the door behind her, heading for the beach. It was a long walk along the stone wall that ran out to sea. Seagulls screeched and the breeze had picked up, throwing white caps up on the waves.

The results had come back. The news was not good. In fact, the news was devastating. Decisions to be made. She had written again to Fiona but had no reply. She was leaving Jenny 'til the weekend. Her side ached and she had not eaten for a day or so because of the endless nausea.

She was trying to be strong and to think positively but she'd never had a big operation before. Dr. Brewer had said he'd like her to go to surgery as soon as possible.

'No time to be wasted,' he'd said. She'd tried to make light of it saying. 'Oh. Prepare to meet thy doom, then?' but he had not been amused. And to be honest, neither was she.

The surgeon had been professional but brusque. Looking like a wild scientist, with grey hair sprouting from all sorts of places on his face and out of his ears, he'd looked at her from under a hedge of eyebrows, saying, 'Well, Mrs. Slade. We won't know it all until we go in. Then all will be revealed, yes? So I'll give you these instructions to prepare you for surgery at the hospital for next Thursday. There's also a letter for you to see the anaesthetist, all right?'

No, not all right. All felt very all wrong. I finally get to connect with my darling Jenny and now this.

She felt the fear come up like a shard of ice from the ground that travelled to the top of her head. A long cold laser light of reality hit home.

It was a tentative knock on the door on Sunday morning that woke Jenny from a deep sleep. She glanced at the clock. Seven thirty. It had been an exhausting shift the night before at the hospital. Her favourite patient had finally been admitted for the last time and had died quietly around midnight. Jenny had stayed on to be with her, as she promised her she would. No family, no friends. Just Jenny and the night nurse. How lonely to die alone, Jenny had thought. No one should go through that. She had sat with Millie 'til her last breath. Holding her hand and stroking her forehead. It had been 1am before she'd got home. Danny was sleeping over at Jai's so the recovery time stretched out luxuriously. She stumbled out of bed on the second knock which was a bit more insistent, grabbing her gown on the way.

Richard stepped back from the door with a gasp, clutching a large paper bag to his chest.

'Oh no. I've picked the wrong moment. I was going to cook us brekkie but I can see...'

Jenny knew how exhausted she looked but didn't bother hiding anything. She drew the old pink gown around her, blinking in the light. 'It's OK. Long night last night at work. Come in anyway.'

She could soon smell the bacon wafting through the house and heard the crash of the back door as Danny came home.

'Hi, Mum. Richard. I'm going to the surf. Had brekkie. See you.'

Usual bullet conversation. And he was off in a flash.

She glanced at Richard. 'I reckon it's months since I had a proper decent conversation with that boy.'

'Don't worry, he'll be bouncing back soon. I was just the same with my mum.'

He threw his arms wide and smiled. 'And look at me now.'

She dressed quickly into jeans and a shirt and dragged herself onto one of the stools at the breakfast bar.

Head resting on her hands she smiled up at Richard.

'Well then,' she said, buttering perfectly browned toast, 'This is a bit of all right.'

'It's a very empty house at my place to be honest. Yours just seemed a great option. Oh, and it's so lovely seeing you. Sorry for waking you. I didn't realise. I forget sometimes about your shift work. My plastering hours are pretty standard compared to yours.'

He foraged around in the cupboards looking for plates and cutlery and Jenny let him, laughing at his attempts.

'Top right. Next to the stove.'

They sat out under the Lilli-Pilli in the old cane chairs. Bees buzzed in the Nasturtiums, yellow on yellow. Jenny and Richard smiled at each other, no words needed, letting out a collective and contented sigh, knowing they were poised on the edge of something.

Putting their empty plates on the ground, they walked back inside to make coffee. Jenny reached out her hand to his, pulling him towards her.

'Thankyou. That's so lovely to have you come and make breakfast.'

His kiss was gentle but intentional. His arms around her felt safe but also excitement began its slow and steady climb. She noticed the flecks of gold amongst the deep brown of his eyes.

'Mmm ... again?' Richard had his eyes closed. She felt herself giving way, giving in, in the loveliest and rightest way imaginable. She closed her eyes and savoured the salty taste of his mouth on hers. Felt the sweet swimming of it. The unexpected yearning.

He pulled away first and leaned on the sink. 'Uh oh. I think we're in danger,' and smiled, his eyes crinkling at the corners, holding her blue gaze for a long time. In a comfortable silence they stacked the dishes and began to clear up the kitchen.

Richard scraped off the last plate into the bin. 'How about we leave these and go out for a drive somewhere?'

The door knock came tentative with a small rat-a-tat-tat.

Jenny marched down the hall way and opened it. She could see the hunched figure of her mother through the stippled glass.

'Mum! What is it? Is something wrong?'

Hermione entered the kitchen completely ignoring Richard at the sink, washing dishes.

'I've got to go to the hospital. Next week. The doctor thinks it's cancer.'

Tears began to course down her face. Jenny didn't move. Wanting to stay but wanting to comfort, and cross at the intrusion, her compassion won out. She went to her mother and put her arms around her in a close hug.

'Come into the lounge, Mum. Sit down and I'll make you a cuppa. It may not be all that bad.'

She rolled her eyes at Richard mouthing, 'Sorry,' to him.

'Look, I'll go and maybe come back a bit later. I've got something I want to show you too.' He gave her a quick kiss and turning at the hallway, smiled into her eyes.

Hermione dried her eyes and blew her nose, accepting the hot tea from Jenny.

'So who's that, Dear?'

'Mum, it's not what it looks like. He just… '

Hermione brightened a little as she glanced down the hall at Richard's departing back. 'Well, what is it then?'

Jenny felt the wall coming up again. Felt her moments stolen.

'He's actually a man I've just started seeing. His wife died a while ago. And Bob is long gone.' She felt herself becoming defensive, and what was becoming a familiar irritation rising.

'Anyway. What's happening with you then?'

CHAPTER 34

The quietness of the operating theatre with just a whoosh of the occasional door and a sound like distant cutlery being moved, was almost stifling. Hermione lay under her hospital gown, too frightened to move, gazing up at the neutral masked staff, into whose hands she was putting her life. The anaesthetist looked incredibly young but gave her a warm smile as he took her arm and checked her veins.

Time was in another dimension and quite out of reach. She woke with a shard of pain like a knife ripping through her abdomen. Glancing round she saw the drip stand with its clear fluid drip-drip dripping into her arm, felt the various tubes and restraints all over her body. She was alone in her room. Heard the squeak of shoes on lino past her room, the hum of the air conditioner, but otherwise the silence. After what seemed an eternity, a large, jolly nurse came in accompanying the surgeon. He picked up the chart at the end of her bed and made some comment to the nurse.

'So. Mrs. Slade. Hermione.' He pronounced it in four syllables. 'How are you doing? You've done well. And so have we, in fact. I'll see you again in the morning and tell you more then.'

He turned on his heel and walked out. Hermione closed her eyes.

CHAPTER 35

Jenny sat munching what was left of a very large Granny Smith apple. Richard sat on the carpet.

Smiling up at her he said, 'Do you seriously eat the core and all? Why do you do that?'

'Always have. Since I was little. Anyway the pips have arsenic or something in it so I won't get cancer, will I?'

Suddenly serious, Richard asked, 'So how is your mum now? After her surgery I mean?'

Jenny frowned. 'I'll go and see her today. This afternoon actually. Come on. Let's have lunch.'

Making meals for Richard was on the normal list now. They were inseparable, but Jenny found she still craved her own space.

When she walked into the hospital ward she breathed in the floor polish, disinfectant and stewed cabbage aroma as familiar to her as a second home. She walked down the corridor to her mother's room. So much more life and hope in the Surgical Wing of the hospital.

Hermione was asleep and looked as white as the bed sheet. Her skin sagged on her and the hospital gown did her no favours. Jenny noticed she had false teeth and they had become dislodged. She sat down quietly and gently touched her mother's arm. 'It's just me, Mum,' she whispered and stroked her hand. 'I've brought you in a couple of nighties for when you're out of this gown.'

Hermione came up from a very deep place almost gasping for air. She opened her eyes and like a drowning woman slipped down into sleep again. A familiar face popped her head around the corner. Julie from Oncology mouthed quietly, 'Sorry to hear about your Mum, Jen.'

Jenny gave a half-smile and raised her eyebrows, waiting for further information.

Julie put her hand over her mouth, startled. 'Oh, you haven't seen the doctor yet have you? Sorry. I'm way out of line.' And she disappeared.

Alerted, Jenny went straight to the Nurses Station desk.

'I need to speak to Dr. Brewer or Dr Stephens. About my mother, Hermione Slade.'

The nurse behind the desk was unsmiling. She handed Jenny the phone and passed the doctor's number to her, returning to her writing immediately.

The news was not good. Liver cancer. Infiltrated the bowel. Basically inoperable. With a deep sigh, Jenny knew exactly what that meant, and what lay ahead for her mum. She sat down beside the bed where her mother slept, unaware. A tenderness towards her mum washed over her and with it a resolution.

Dawn broke out with a fanfare of pinks and golds, announcing the day. Ghost crabs scurried home after finishing their night shift. The ocean dipped and plunged, steely grey in fresh light. A few sea gulls strutted proudly on silver sand, bright and beady eyed.

Hermione sat hunched on a park bench looking out to sea and a new day dawning. She winced as she moved her legs under the rug covering her dress. The wound was healing now, six weeks on. Dr. Brewer had been very kind but his words hung in the air between them.

'It's not good, Hermione, but let's hope for the best.'

Whatever time is left, she thought, I owe it to my girls. If they'll have me. She pulled the newspaper clipping from her pocket and re-read it. She knew exactly what she had to do.

The sun came up, blazing gold. The dog walkers began their parade along the water's edge, throwing sticks and shouting commands. The interruption rattled her daze and with a supreme effort she managed to get up and walk back to her own place. Breathing heavily, she reached into the bathroom cabinet for more pain killers. The little weather board house divided into flats, as dismal as it was, had become her haven over the last few months, even though she had had to give up the real estate job. It was good being in Bunjip. Maybe the last stop now. Gideon Vale, although only a half hour drive, seemed another world away and one she chose to ignore. For now.

She threw down the bitter tasting pills with a shudder and sat watching the noisy Miners in the red Grevilleas, cheeping like crazy. She turned the letter to Fiona over and over in her hands, and, like a child, wrote on the back SWALK. With a smile, she planted a kiss on the envelope and popped it in her handbag. The pain killers took their time but as soon as 9 o'clock came she walked out of the flat locking the door and walked to the bus stop nearby, dropping the envelope into the post box on the way. The sun shimmered like a wattle blossom in a watery sky. In spite of the early summer heat she felt cold in her sundress that now swam on her frail body. She drew her pink cardigan around her shoulders and sat patiently. The bus took the longest possible route, passing the Ti Tree lake and trundling into Eden Estate. She watched a flock of ducks veering across the lake as the sun climbed higher in the watercolour sky.

Jenny's house was only a hundred yards or so from where she alighted. It felt like a long journey. Her hands trembled somewhat at what she had to say to Jenny but she walked resolutely to her front door. The door was already open and the sun poured through the hallway to greet her.

'There, Jen?' her voice echoed through the house. Barney, the ginger cat wiggled towards her, his tail an orange plume. She started to bend down to pat him but found the pain too much. She called through the house and heard a faint sound coming from the garden. Barney followed her, sniffing the air.

'Out here, Mum. Planting my bulbs.'

She made her way out to the garden where the Lilli-Pilli dripped its jelly-bean berries and all the flower beds were showing off their colour. Gerberas stood in stately array all pinks and reds while blue and pink salvias competed for attention. Pick me! Pick me! Across to the side the vegie garden was a burst of green health with lettuces, rocket and broccoli in tidy rows.

'Wow,' said Hermione as she collapsed with a sigh onto the cane chair, 'You've done a fabulous job, Jen, all on your own.'

Jen wiped her muddy hands on her shorts, shaking a wisp of hair out of her eyes. 'Well, Richard helped do the heavy digging it must be said. Credit where it's due.' Jenny smiled across at her mother, then frowning, saw how exhausted she was.

'Did you catch the bus? I've said I'll always come and pick you up in the car. I'm getting you a cuppa, Mum. Stay right there. Comfortable enough?'

Hermione nodded, smiling a thank you, overwhelmed at the kindness of her daughter. Guilt wrapped its cold arms around her yet again.

'Sorry, darling, to put you to this trouble.' And she rested back on the cushions of the cane chair, exhausted from the effort of travel and arrival. Sleep came quickly.

Jenny came out with a tray of tea in a brown teapot with cups rattling and a jug of milk.

'Darjeeling, Mum. Leaf, not bag.' Sometimes Jenny felt that no time had elapsed in their relationship.

Hermione loved what she called "a proper tray of tea." Jenny had been feeling her heart soften hugely towards her mum since Richard had waltzed into her life. It was a win all round.

Hermione sat up wearily. She checked that the clipping was still in her pocket folded neatly.

She smiled with gratitude at Jenny. 'Thank you, pet. Perfect.'

They sipped their tea together as if they'd been doing this for thirty years. If only. Hermione looked with undisguised pleasure at her daughter's sky blue eyes and long fair hair, her suntanned legs in their little denim shorts. All those missed birthdays and graduations. The tears began to spill out again as she travelled the downward spiral of hating herself for her absence.

Jenny reached over and took her hand and looked right into her eyes, now awash. 'Mum. It's OK. I do forgive you, you know.' She squeezed her thin, bony hand. 'You're here now. That's what matters. Fiona has to work her part out herself.'

Hermione sniffed, grabbing her hanky from her pocket, dropping the clipping onto the grass.

'I don't deserve you, Jen. I really don't. Thank you.'

Jenny reached down and picked up the clipping, giving it back to her mother.

'Which ... which brings me to something I want to ask you.'

She handed the clipping to Jenny to read. Jenny's face softened and she smiled as she read the clipping.

'Would you come with me to this? It would mean so much...' her voice trailed off.

'The ballet. Sydney.' Jenny got up from her chair and knelt in front of her mother's chair, gently putting her arms around her. Her own tears began.

'Of course, Mum. I'd love to. But I'm not sure if...' her voice trailed off.

She pulled back and smiled into Hermione's eyes. She saw a small frail woman, a shadow of herself, battling cancer and the march of time, trying very hard to recoup the losses. She was grateful that Bob had departed the scene, that Hermione had never had to be at the brunt of his sarcasm and aggression. Peace prevailed in her home. Danny was a happier teenager, if a bit distant, but nothing untoward for his age and stage. Puberty blues as they called it. He now had a grandmother, albeit for a short time. A wave of gratitude washed over her in a deeper sense than she had ever felt.

CHAPTER 36

It was a lazy Tuesday morning and the beach-front was quiet, stretching itself out like a relaxed cat in the sun. A picture postcard sort of day, without apology. A few couples walked holding hands along the sea wall, the waves pounding against the rocks sending up a foamy spray onto the path, causing them to jump back with a squeal. Sea gulls shrieked, wheeling in the sea breeze. The red and white awnings shook and rippled.

Jenny sat with Caroline at the Café Bernard, the new café. Done out with French style everything, along with Impressionist paintings on the wall, it at least had some atmosphere that wasn't all about the surf.

Caroline had her wise-owl face on and leaned across the table to Jenny. 'Enjoy this, Jen. Don't rush it. Don't give everything but don't give nothing.'

She sat back in her chair, arms folded, waiting for Jenny's response. Is she talking about me and Mum? Or me and Richard? Both applied.

Jenny nodded. 'How do you know all this stuff, Darl? Yep. You're right, of course.'

Caroline brightened up and sat bolt upright.

'Yes, I am. And by the way I'm studying Pysch now at the Uni. Always wanted to do that. I'm practising on you to be honest.' She threw back her head laughing.

Jenny's gaze was steady. 'No, you're not. Find another guinea pig. No. Just kidding. I need all the help I can get what with Mum now and this whole thing with Richard...'

'So? And? The problem is...?'

Jenny twisted her serviette into a long screwy roll. Without looking up she said, 'Look, I just don't know if I really deserve a guy like Rich. I mean Bob used to say...'

Caroline banged her cup down a little too hard and rolled her eyes.

'Oh, for heaven's sake, Jen. Not this again. Wake up! Rich is a great guy but you are so enough for him. Danny's a lovely boy 'cos you're such a good mum. So, your mum walked out on you. Her loss. Bob was such a drop kick he never even saw you. Your whole life is about to happen.'

Jenny looked up and smiled at her friend. She leaned across the table and squeezed her hand.

'Thanks Caroline. I'm so lucky to have you.'

Suddenly, the door was flung open as a gust of wind propelled Richard into the café. He walked towards the two women, waving a bunch of papers in the air.

'Hey, girls, I've got a great idea.' His voice went into a stage whisper as he glanced around the almost empty café. 'I'm going to look at the health food shop round the corner. It's up for grabs.'

He showed them the papers with pictures of a drab, brown shop front.

'That's great, Rich,' Jenny smiled at his excitement. 'When can you see it?'

'Right away actually. Here's hoping.' He held up crossed fingers.

Caroline smiled at them both and quickly finished her coffee. 'I'll let you two love birds celebrate. I've got an assignment to write.' She stood up and left the café, door slamming behind her.

'What's up with her?' asked Richard, frowning

'Nothing I know about. Maybe she's jealous. I dunno. Maybe she always had the hots for you. Too late now though, hey?' She grabbed his hand and kissed it.

Richard smiled. 'Listen, you. Caroline's OK, but well ... you know, too bossy for my liking.' He put his arm around her and drew her in close. 'It's you I want. No one else. Okay? Anyway. Let's celebrate. Chinese tonight? Danny too, of course. He loves it.'

He stood and went to leave. 'Wanna see this place? I've got the keys.'

Jenny shook her head. 'Oh, I'd so love to but sorry, Rich. Work calls. Need to leave soon. Tell me all about it tonight.'

He walked out quickly, throwing her a kiss at the door, leaving Jenny in the silence of the now-empty café. She leaned back in her chair and finished her coffee and thought about Sydney and the ballet. And how much it meant to her. She hoped her mother would be up to it in her recovery.

The trip down south was long and arduous. Hermione did her level best to be positive and mother-y. It was obvious even to the untrained eye that Hermione was gravely ill and in pain. An hour from the city Jen pulled the car over.

'Mum. We don't have to do this you know. I'm a big girl now.'

She took a deep breath and stared through the windscreen of the car into the dusk light. 'I'll be really straight with you. Yes, it broke my heart waiting for you that day when you never came back. I had my hopes set on the ballet. Of course I did. Some things though, you can't just, well, repeat. Plus, mum, I work with patients with cancer all the time. I know this is hard for you.'

Hermione leaned over and grabbed her hand. Her face was sunken and pale with exhaustion and pain. Her voice was hoarse and strained. 'C'mon girl. We are doing this. Might be the last time.' She closed her eyes and slept.

A few spots of rain spat at the windscreen. The road rolled out like a slick, black carpet under the swish of the wheels. As they approached the city and its forest of glittery lights, Jenny knew that nothing could turn back the clock but this was more important to her mum than to her. The nurse part of her thought it was a crazy trip but as Hermione's daughter, abandoned on the fence waiting to go to the ballet as a ten year old, she saw the importance as part of a long-awaited reconciliation. She pulled out onto the highway and let her thoughts ramble around like so many marbles in a bowl. Her mother slept, mouth open, looking like death.

What did she actually remember of her mum before the day her world changed? She had always believed that she and Fiona were not enough for her mum to stay. She thought of how impossible it would be to even entertain the possibility of leaving Danny. How does a mother do that? Was it total selfishness? Boredom? She wasn't even enough for Bob to love and to cherish. What's cherishing about? Maybe Richard would get bored and leave as well? The downward spiral of negative thought spun in her head. The memories of childhood began to surface. They collided against each other like apples in a bucket of water.

A memory hit like a wave in the dark. She had been sick in bed and her mum took her into the big bed and read her The Velveteen Rabbit. The next day she was better and her mum let her stay home another day and they read books together and coloured in. She remembered the bear her mum had made on a rare sewing exploit. It was made from a brown wool skirt with black buttons for eyes. She smiled as the picture recreated.

There were blanks and spaces, leavings and absences. Shouting and silences in the drab grey house where her father moved like a shadow amongst the debris of their lives, walking on the eggs her mother laid down like a minefield. Like a bolt from the blue, she realised that living with Bob had been like that too. Studying his moods, his silences, reading the weather of his day.

The exhaustion of it all.

Truth came, hard and clean: my mother loved me while she was there. Just not enough to stay.

She glanced over at the frown crossing Hermione's face, checking how far away the Theatre was.

She had booked them into a motel quite near the Opera House. The sky was inky black and full of stars blinking back approval. They both dollied up as the time to go drew closer. The Opera House was not a disappointment. Its great white iconic sails against the night sky were breathtaking to them both. As the curtain went up and the first strains of the orchestra swept over them, Hermione came to life and they were both entranced. It ended all too soon. The bitter sweetness of loss and regaining was not lost on either of them.

The drive home the next day was gruelling for Hermione. Every bone ached and Jenny had to stop frequently just so her mother could have some respite from the jolting of the car. Finally she pulled up outside her mum's flat. All the windows were closed on the block of flats. A couple of magpies chortled on the old broken wire fence. A few unopened newspapers gathered at the fence line and the mail box was overflowing onto the weed-infested ground underneath. Jenny looked across at her mother, gaunt and pale. Hermione made a move to get out of the car.

'Give me the key, mum. I want you to come home with me.'

Hermione opened her eyes trying to adjust to the glare of the day. She began to protest, putting her hand up like a stop sign, then laid it back down again.

'Yes, Dear. Yes. That'd be lovely.' She sank back to sleep again.

CHAPTER 37

Racquel Easte stood in front of the desk at the Railway Booking Office. Long straight black hair framed an alabaster complexion in a face that was not quite pretty but not unattractive. Her dark eyes under beautifully arched eyebrows looked steadily at the girl behind the counter.

'No, it's not Rachel. It's Racquel, like Racquel Welch.' The girl looked puzzled. 'You know, the movie actress?'

The girl chewed the end of her biro. 'Spell, please.'

Everyone called her Rachel but she was always adamant about her name. Her birth mother, she knew, had called her Rachel. Sometimes just to be different she used her second name, Louise.

Finally the day was here that she had longed for but also feared like nothing else in her life. She had isolated what the fears were and the people at the Agency had been brilliant.

'Don't place your expectations too high on birth parents,' they had advised. 'Particularly a first meeting. You'll set yourself up for a fall otherwise.'

All of her 22 years she had wondered about her actual biological birth mum and dad. The what, the who and more importantly the why of her adoption. She understood the 70s and all that went with it to some degree. The social status quo and how many babies had been given away with little or no support for single mums back then. She had been an angry, dissociated teenager, running with the rebels and loving their take on life, smoking joints and drinking beer every weekend, hanging in the sandhills, watching their boyfriends ride the waves down on the Southern Rocks, right up 'til the sun went down and you couldn't see your hand in front of you. Somehow she'd managed to finish school with a reasonable mark, even able to get into Uni to study her passion: Arts History.

Trish and Pete Easte had adored her from the moment they held her as a tiny bundle of squall at the hospital nursery. It had been a long wait for their moment. They had been pastors out in the hard-core Western Suburbs for seven years now, and were pure gold really. No babies for them.

They had always told her the truth from when she was a tiny girl, her big brown eyes staring trustingly up at Trish and Pete's faces as they read her stories at bedtime, telling her that she had been selected and picked and that God had always known her name and had put her together and sent her from heaven. Pretty cool idea, she had always thought. She had come out of her wild teen years and morphed into a teetering adulthood, still searching for the missing parts of her identity that didn't quite fit the rest of her.

One of her girlfriends said to her once, 'There's something really Celtic about you, Racquel. The way you love Irish dance and music and stuff.'

She had stopped praying about those endless questions and missing answers a long time ago but it sure felt like an answer to her prayers when the A4 manilla envelope arrived in the mail, post marked Bunjip Bay. Where the heck was that? And then the "what ifs" began. All of them anchored in rejection or at least the fear of it. So here it was, several letters later, a part of the flag beginning to unfurl, the last piece of the puzzle being put in place at last. There was an excitement too, like the biggest-ever firecracker ever invented, ready to go off inside her, at just the thought of meeting actual bloodline relatives. Or at least people close to the bloodline.

She paid her fare after leaning right over the counter, checking that her name was spelt correctly. Names were so important.

'Thank you,' she said with measured tone to the girl who did not look up but twirled a brown curl near her mouth.

Racquel turned with a flourish, leaving the door wide open. It was a short walk down to the platform and she boarded quickly. A window seat on her own. Four hours. Her thoughts raced away like streamers in a wind. She settled back indulging in the luxury of a new magazine.

CHAPTER 38

Six weeks earlier

Richard didn't bother to knock anymore. He wandered down the hallway of the old timber house calling Jenny's name. The room Hermione occupied had the door slightly open. He glimpsed Danny in his room, radio blaring, hunched over some music sheets. Richard had lashed out and bought him an acoustic guitar. Danny had been elated.

Richard gave him a quick poke in the ribs and laughed as he jumped. 'G'day mate. How's it going?' and kept walking into the kitchen where Jenny stood in her usual blue jeans and T shirt making pancakes. She turned around and put her arms out to him, snuggling into his neck, breathing in his salty-earthy smell.

'Just in time. Pancakes? Maple syrup and ice cream? Danny's favourite. And yours, of course.'

'You got me, Girl,' he said and put the brown manila envelope on the bench.

'You've got that envelope again. Must be something important? What's in it?'

Richard frowned and put his arm around her shoulders.

'I need to share something with you. After brekkie will do.'

Jenny shrugged and kept flipping pancakes. She was nervy today. Gut full of bats flapping. Only yesterday she'd flipped out again as old triggers shot up her old anxiety. She had been looking after a newly arrived patient, a man about fifty. He had come staggering out of the bathroom, his gown flapping around his thin legs. In pain he had shouted at her, 'Get me some pain killers. You stupid nurse can't you see I'm in trouble here?'

She had run out of the room shaking with a thundering heart. Ran into an empty room as it spun all around her and thought she would pass out. It took minutes for her to calm and settle and for the shaking to stop.

What's wrong with me? Can't even do my job now.

Relaxed now in her own kitchen, with Richard lazily spinning around on the swivel stool, she smiled at the memory, knowing she was being hard on herself. As usual.

She called Danny and they ate in the garden, dribbling maple syrup over rapidly melting ice cream on plate-sized pancakes. Flies began to buzz about. They drank their tea in big steaming mugs. Danny went off to his room mumbling about homework to be done and Jenny and Richard were left to themselves.

'You're nervous as a cat. What is it? C'mon. Out with it.' Jenny sensed the change in the atmosphere. Somewhere in the house a door slammed.

'Looks like rain. Veranda?'

They took their tea to the old bamboo chairs on the side of the house, sheltered from the weather. Covered in Wisteria vines and Jasmine in the spring time, it was Jenny's favourite place to be alone.

Richard sighed a deep sigh. 'OK, here goes.' He screwed up his eyes and took a deep breath.

'Look, there was a baby. I mean there is...'

Jenny was immediately on guard and sat up straight. 'What do you mean there is...?'

'I've got to get this story out, Jen. It's important for us both. It's about Bob.'

He hesitated and with a deep breath, looked up at her face. 'And Marilyn. Way back. Before us.'

The story unfolded itself. Jenny sat chewing her top lip for a while. Still and quiet, she stared through the railings at her garden. She hardly dared breathe.

'Dear God. Hang on a sec. Bob never said a word. Nothing.' She looked at Richard. 'And by the look of it, it was news to you. How long have you known?'

'Marilyn told me just before she died. She made her peace with it all but was so, so sad she never got to see her own daughter. That's the next important bit.' He took a shuddery breath. 'She has made contact. The daughter, that is. Now she wants to meet us.'

Jenny clasped her face in her hands. 'Hang on. Hang on. What? She's coming here? When?'

'Look ... soon. Ish. If it's OK with you? The way I see it, this poor girl has a right to put some pieces together. I think I might know how you feel and so do I. But Danny has a half-sister. Your mum has a sort of grandchild. I've got copies of all the documents here. Her name is Racquel. As in Welch. You know...'

'Yes, I know. The movie star.' Jenny chewed the side of her thumb.

They looked at each other in silence. Richard spoke first. 'No secrets, you said. Well, here's a doozy of a one for us. I know it's a shock. I've known for a lot longer than you and yeah, I was pretty angry I wasn't told too. Funny thing though. Marilyn finally told me she called the baby Rachel. Close enough, I reckon. I had always thought it was my problem. You know. No kids.'

'I think this calls for a beach walk. Let's take Danny too. I'll tell him there.'

Danny was happy to leave the home work behind, sensing a different atmosphere. They told him in the car on the drive to the Seven Mile. He threw back his head and groaned. Then with a very large smile said, 'Hey guys. I've got a sister.'

There had been letters back and forth between Racquel, Richard and Jenny for quite a few weeks and they had all decided it was a good idea to meet. Hermione had been included in it all and was so grateful to be part of it. Danny was probably the most excited of all of them. The 10.20 from Sydney had never been so eagerly awaited. It was also curiosity that made Richard and Jenny keen to see what the progeny of Bob and Marilyn would be like.

Jenny felt it was like the daughter she never had but didn't want to get carried away with sentimentality.

The train pulled into the small town station. One carriage door opened. A tall, elegant young woman with long black hair and an intentional chin stepped onto the platform. Her skin was Irish white and her eyes were deep brown. She had navy slacks with small, heeled patent-leather shoes and a matching blazer with silver buttons. There was no hesitation. This was Bob's daughter. With a polite and restrained hug all round, they drove home in Richard's car. Jenny hardly dared look at her. Expensive perfume wafted around the car. Collective anxiety engulfed them.

Hermione met them at the door, her green flowery gown almost engulfing her in its now too-large folds.

'Come in, come in. Welcome home. It's so lovely to see you, Dear,' and she enfolded Racquel in her arms.

So much to say. So much left unsaid.

Richard went home after a cup of tea, promising to pick Racquel up later in the afternoon to show her Marilyn's photos and keepsakes that had been put aside for her. Danny promised to show her his surfing skills. Hermione sat quietly watching the scene unfold. Well, well. I do have a family. Quite undeserved but lovely, she thought.

Racquel and Jenny flowed into each other's hearts like two streams. Jenny kept Bob's history as light as possible, showing her photos of what appeared constantly to be an unhappy and angry man. Even on their wedding day he was scowling. Jenny looked wistfully at her. 'You've got his eyes, his colouring. I'd have almost picked you out in a crowd.' They smiled at each other. Marilyn's wide and lovely smile, for sure.

'What do you do in Sydney now?'

Racquel flicked her hair back and put her head on the side, exactly the way Bob used to.

'Well, I did an Arts History major at Uni and I work in a gallery in Sydney called, Elan Elan. It specialises in supplying art works to big hotels all round the world, so I'm actually a consultant for them. I go into places where people don't really have a clue and choose pieces that will go with décor, position and architecture. I love it, actually. A lot of travel.'

She glanced around Jenny's almost bare walls with nothing but photos of Danny surfing, Danny as a boy. No sign of Bob. No sign of Jenny and Bob.

Jenny topped up their tea from the pot. 'Wow, that's amazing. Got a favourite?'

'Well, you'll probably laugh but my favourite is Sir John Lavery. Funnily enough he's a famous Irish painter. I always loved his stuff even before I knew my heritage. Must be in the genes,' she said with a laugh. They were easy with each other.

Richard picked her up in the afternoon and took her back to his house. Its emptiness was tangible. The shutters on the veranda hung clattering as a steady sea breeze blew in from the front. The garden was overgrown with weeds and a few newspapers littered the front. They sat in the lounge with its faded blue chairs while Richard went down the hall and came back with a large cardboard box with a white label on it that you could just about make out the inscription, Rachel.

Racquel took the box from Richard. 'My mother.' The word hung in the air like a key waiting. She held the box very tenderly. 'May I take this with me, then? I don't ... I don't think I can do this right now.'

Richard sat down gently on the arm of the lounge chair. 'It's yours, Racquel. All yours. Have it. Take as long as you need. There is a birthday card for you for every year since the day you were born. She, she always loved you. I'm sorry. I don't really know what...'

Racquel touched his arm. 'It's OK. Really. I just need time. It's a heck of a lot to take in.' She looked over to the sideboard where a framed photo of Marilyn stood. Young, vibrant, happy and looking into the camera lens with just the same expression as her daughter.

'She's beautiful.' She smiled up at him. ' You must miss her.'

Richard smiled. Neither of them looked at the other. 'I do. But it's getting easier.' He got up quickly and crossed to the picture of Marilyn. 'Ask me anything you want. I only wish I'd known...'

Racquel picked up the box, sensing its incredible value. No piece of art in the world could replace the treasure she held in her hands. She placed it carefully in a large plastic bag and went to Richard's car. It was a silent journey as they drove to the motel where she was staying for the night.

The Pink Flamingo Motel flashed its neon welcome as Richard pulled up out the front. Racquel walked into her room and placed the box on the bed. Exhausted she discarded her jacket and lay across the bed. And let the tears fall.

The finality was overwhelming. Emotions rushed at her like ghosts from history. The room was suddenly too small, too intense, with its cheap faded Matisse prints all around the wall. She threw off her city clothes, her nice patent-leather heels and stockings and felt the unfamiliar sensation of floor on bare feet.

Finding a beach shift she dragged it on and leaving the box in the middle of the bed unopened, walked out into a darkening night. She could hear the beckoning of the sea thundering in the distance and made her way towards the sound. The sand felt foreign to her, an unstable substance underfoot. A brisk ocean breeze lifted her dark hair off her neck as she breathed the salty air. She twirled around in circles like a child and threw her head back laughing. Ghost crabs scuttled as evening crept in. The beach was empty of people, the only sound the roar of waves. She felt an unexpected and overwhelming sense of completeness and begun to run, her bare feet thudding rhythmically into damp sand, water curling around her ankles. She ran beyond the lights of the town, the beach lit only by a rising pale moon.

She thought of her birth parents, both gone now. Weighed the effect of her presence now on this new family, who seemed nice enough but had their own reminiscences to pick through. Felt a belonging somewhere in a larger sense, an extended sense. Maybe. Just maybe. And a gorgeous half-brother!

She sat, slightly puffed out, on a sand bank and watched the moon make a path out to sea leaving a pale golden stair. A couple of heads bobbed along the shore line, rods over their shoulders. She relaxed against the sand, the wind picking up a bit now, blowing her long straight hair across her face. Glancing at her watch she slowly got to her feet and began the trek back to Bunjip.

There's always tomorrow, she thought as she crossed the sand towards the town lights.

Chapter 39

Jenny threw the sheet off her again and tried to read the time on the luminescent clock on the crowded bedside table, knocking off a book onto the floor with a loud bang. Only 3am. Thoughts whirled around her mind, chased by feelings she wished she never had. Anger surfaced from a deep place. Talk about a dark secret. Talk about a dark horse. And here she was. This lovely girl. Beautiful and full of life. Not the dark secretive eyes of Bob but sparkling joyous windows on a world that was full of hope and future.

Racquel had stayed with them for the long weekend and was going back this morning. Back to the city. To an exciting job surrounded by beauty and art. She sort of fitted, this new daughter. So much in common with the four of them. Even Hermione had sparked up and been attentive, until the pain kicked in.

Racquel had gone down to the beach and watched Danny surfing. Even had a go herself and laughed at her mistakes. Had them all laughing. So different from Bob. Richard had watched her walking along the beach with Danny, both of them laughing together.

'You may not believe me, Jen, but she actually walks exactly like Marilyn did.'

He shook his head in disbelief. 'You know, the way she throws her right foot.'

Jenny had to agree. Genetics were a peculiar thing.

The three of them took her to the station. The hugs were genuine. The sharp sound of Racquel's heels ricocheted off the empty station walls. Just before the doors closed, she turned and waved, throwing a kiss.

Richard shut the passenger door and got in the driver's side. With his hands on the wheel he turned round to Danny in the back.

'So. Whaddya reckon, Mate ?'

'Yep. She's nice. I like her.' He gave a nervous laugh, 'No good at surfing, but.'

Richard put his hand over Jenny's. 'How you doing, Love?'

'Dunno. Mixed bag really.' She turned away and looked out the window. 'Maybe later?'

'Sure. Let's see how the old girl's going then.'

'Yeah. Mum. My mum.' Jen smiled as she said the words.

Hermione was asleep in the spare room that Jenny had made up for her. There were boxes piled into corners and half of the pink floral curtain was falling off the rail. It was the best she could do for now, though.

'Just 'til you're better,' she had said hopefully.

The letter addressed to Hermione had arrived that morning and sat unopened on the hallstand. Jenny turned it over and read with surprise her sister's name and address. Arching her eyebrows, she took it into her mother's room and placed it on the bedside table. Light shone in shafts through the partially closed curtains.

She tiptoed around her mother's bed but Hermione remained deeply asleep. Jenny drew up close to her mother's face, looking intently as if to discover some hidden truth.

She straightened up and left the room in a rush, catching her blank face in the hall mirror. Hurrying into her uniform, she grabbed her watch and drove to the Hospital.

It was just as busy as ever that afternoon. IV infusions to start, relatives to comfort. The usual paper work. Around 10.30, Megan, one of the nurses came towards her with the phone.

'It's Richard. He sounds worried.'

She grabbed the phone from Megan, and breathless, asked, 'What's wrong, Darl?'

There was panic in his voice. 'It's your mum. I can't wake her. I can't ... I don't...'

'OK. I'll get off now and come straight home. Don't panic. Might need to call an ambulance.'

The car flew through Bunjip Bay, taking the corners too fast. She slammed the car door and ran into the house.

'Mum. Mum. Wake up.' She shook her gently. Nothing. Fiona's letter sat unopened on the bedside table.

Hermione was unconscious. Her pale gaunt face and frail body said it all. Richard and Danny came and stood next to her, waiting for the decision. Jenny rang the ambulance then packed a few nighties and her mother's toiletries.

Soon she was a patient in the Oncology ward. Jenny sat beside the bed alone, holding her mother's hand.

'But I haven't said what I need to say.'

A soft yellow glow shone under the door and she could hear the quiet chat of the night staff.

She looked down at her mother's weary face and felt compassion properly, for the first time. Saw her as a woman who had simply looked for love and for happiness. Felt the anger and pain wash out of her like a tide.

She began tentatively. 'Mum, I don't know if you can hear me or not. But I need to say these words. These things. When ... when you left, my world came to an end. So did Dad's and Fiona's. We didn't know what to do. Where you'd gone. I'm only just starting to forgive you for that. But it's OK. It's all right now. Danny's my darling boy and then there's Richard. You never met Bob. You'd have hated him, Mum. Bad choice I know. I know that now. You and I can't get the years back but to be honest, I got used to not having you round. And Mum ... you can let go now. I'm letting you go.'

She laid her head down next to Hermione's and kissed her cheek. Her breathing was shallow and intermittent. She saw the light change as the door behind her opened, and she felt the comfort of Richard's arms and then noticed Danny standing at the door.

'It's OK, Darling. Just say goodbye. Your Grandma's not got long now.'

Danny walked slowly over and patted Hermione's arm. His face was ashen. In a few shallow breaths she was gone. The stillness filled the room.

It was two o'clock in the morning before they all got home. Barney the ginger cat met them in the driveway, his tail waving in the cold night air. Exhausted, Jenny went one last time into her mother's room. One small suitcase with barely any evidence that Hermione had lived a life at all. Suddenly remembering Fiona, she ripped the unopened letter from her sister and scanned the lines. It was a long and bitter letter with lots of pages and every page was a loaded gun. Breath whistled from Jenny's mouth. 'Thank God, she never got to read this.'

She went to the phone to let Fiona know of their mother's passing. A sleepy voice answered

'Hi Fiona, it's me, Jen. I'm sorry, Love, but Mum has passed away. Just tonight. I've just got home.' There was silence at the end of the line. 'Are you there, Fi? Are you OK?'

'God, I didn't even get over to see her. Well. Well. Well.'

'Look, let's talk tomorrow. I'm exhausted. I just wanted to...'

'Yeah. Yeah. OK.' And the phone went dead. She sat looking at it as if it were a grenade, then placed it back in the cradle with a very deep sigh. She realised how deeply bone weary she was. She thought back to the little girl who had waited and waited all afternoon on the fence and felt the weight of what she had never had with her mother. Every good mark at school, every excelling moment, the teen years of confusion and loneliness. Her wedding. Miscarriages and no mum for comfort. And then, there was Bob.

She went into Danny's room and sat on the edge of his bed. A rush of love overwhelmed her as she saw how small and vulnerable he looked.

'So, Mum ... why did she leave?'

'Oh, Darling, she was really sick...'

'No. I mean before. Ages ago. When you were little.'

'Oh. That. Look, she met someone else when she was married to my Dad. It happens sometimes.'

'But that's, well ... that's just awful. She left for all these years. She left you and Fiona .'

'I know. I got used to it. We all did. And yes, it was hard and sometimes I think I hated her for it. Now go to sleep. It's been a long night.'

She stroked his forehead, brushing his long blond fringe off his eyes and freckly nose. As she turned the light off and went to leave the room, Danny sat up in bed.

'Mum. That was really nice you got to see her and take her back, even into our house.'

Jenny smiled. 'You never stop wanting your mum to love you, Darling. Now, go to sleep. I love you.'

Jenny, overtired now, lay down on the new lounge and put the TV on low. Flicked through the channels but found nothing outside horror and gore. She lay in the dark, processing the evening. The wind came up, flapping some loose branches against the window. Feeling the sudden aloneness, the tears came. She wept for what could never be, what was and the small moments they had enjoyed together. And relief as well. Another funeral. Every one she had ever loved had left her. One way or another. The risk of love. Enormous. And now here was Richard. Only a matter of time and circumstance.

Sleep came towing her out of the shallows and into the deep places of oblivion.

CHAPTER 40

The funeral was embarrassingly small. What an end to a life unlived. Fiona didn't even bother to travel over from Perth.

'What's the point, Jen? When did she ever do anything for me?'

Jenny left it at that, grateful for the months she had had with her Mum. No regrets. Fiona could wait.

After the funeral Jenny began to take an assessment of her life. Caroline was always asking her what she really, really wanted to do.

She had seen the job advertised in the Sydney papers. Got the new qualification now and was so ready for a change. She had majored in PTSD counselling and felt that life had taught her a lot, all thanks to Bob in a weird way. Maybe life on her own would be less complicated. It would free Richard to find someone with less baggage.

She filled out the application form and mailed it off. Deadline. Tuesday. Her nights were filled with the pros and cons and to-ing and fro-ing of her mind, agonising over whether she'd even get an interview. The possibility of a move away from all she knew and loved. A new school for Danny.

The letter arrived in a brown official-looking manila envelope. She drove down for the interview, half hoping not to get it. Her new grey suit with her crisp white shirt made her feel adequate for whatever lay ahead.

The panel of three men with closed faces and one woman with a mask-of-spackle make up was daunting to say the least. During the interview, after discussing qualifications and schooling, one of the men had asked her point blank if she had ever experienced PTSD personally. She lifted her head and looked at him, her heart racing.

'Oh yes. I was married to a violent man. I know what it's like. It's about living with the threat of death.'

He cleared his throat and looked away. 'Any questions you want to ask the panel?'

Jenny realised in that moment she really wanted this job. Imagined being able to help other women through their panic attacks and anxiety.

'Just one. When does the job become available?'

'After Christmas. We do have a branch operating quite near...' he squinted down at her application form, 'Bunyip Bay, is it?' He pronounced it as if it was a foreign word in a foreign place and wrinkled his nose in distaste.

Jenny smiled. 'Bunjip. With a 'j'. It's an Aboriginal word.'

'We'll let you know. Thank you for coming in.'

The woman smiled at her in a conspiratorial way. She knew all right. Jennifer stood up, dropping all her papers and knocking the chair over with a clatter onto the polished floor. The woman whose name was Jane she remembered, hurried round to her side and quietly picked the chair up and grabbed all her papers. The men looked down at their notes, ignoring the entire incident.

She was dismissed. She heard the hydraulic pfffft hiss of the closing door. With a gut of stone and pounding heart, she left the building and hurried to the café downstairs outside the office building.

I want this.

She looked up at the square of blue sky between the concrete high rises towering overhead.

Quietly sipping a cappuccino, the city now a background noise, she thought about the job. Already a couple of the nurses at work had confided in her about their own abuse at home. They had just felt that Jen would understand. A knowing between some women. Collaborative somehow. Secrets and lies kept hidden from the prying eyes of the rest of the voyeurs. Some things could never be told. She was good at keeping secrets. Remembered the shame at school when her mother left the family. The whispers and stolen glances. Learned early to keep her mouth shut and share nothing.

Chapter 41

It had been the usual busy afternoon shift on the Oncology ward, Chemo patients in and out, patient discharges and still more admissions. Jenny and Megan worked together well, stripping beds and remaking them. Megan was a striking-looking redhead with long curly hair and an alabaster skin like a pre-Raphaelite painting. Nervous as a colt with those huge, startled blue eyes. As they put the final touches to the blue hospital-logoed quilt, Jenny stood up and leaning towards Megan reached out her hand to Megan's hair.

'Hang on. What's that in your hair ? It looks like...' she gasped.

Meagan flushed to the roots as Jenny reached up, pulling out a string of pink.

She drew her breath in with a sob.

'It's meat. It's mince. I, I was late home with the groceries and I had a pound of mince, and Gary...' she broke off with a sob.

Jenny was wide eyed and furious

'Do you mean your husband put this through your hair?'

Meagan nodded and leaned against the wall in embarrassment with deep groaning sobs. 'I know what you're thinking. I can't go. I've got the kids to think about. Mum won't have us.'

Seething, Jenny quietly shut the door and went to Megan, putting her arms around her and shushing her like a child.

The rest of the day was a blur. Jenny was a woman on a mission.

It was late afternoon when she went alone to the Seven Mile and sat high up in the dunes. Still reeling from what Megan had shared as well as other stories from other women at work, she looked out to the metallic-grey sea, its sad, lonely sound pushing to shore.

She thudded her hand on the dampening sand, 'Something must be done.'

It was only this week she had read about the first recognised Women's Shelter opening in Sydney. Out of necessity, of course. She understood what set women off who had come out of abusive marriages even years later. So many triggers. Women like her. Like Megan. Like Evelyn. Women without choices, family or income. Women who had to steal from their sleeping or drunken husbands' trouser pockets to get food for the kids. Women who were secreted away from family, friends, even towns, beaten and subjugated to all sorts. No mums around. It was triggers like loud angry voices, slamming doors, being in a confined space with a man, sudden noises. Never mind the back seats of cars. Jenny knew them all. Enough to send you off like a blithering, shaking idiot back into some lurking memory that won't die let alone be buried. Feelings buried alive that won't shut up. She knew the hyper-vigilance of light sleep, knowing how to lock the doors quickly anywhere in the house. Grab the kids, quick. Ready, always ready for the getaway if needed.

She was ashamed to admit she was waiting for Richard to turn like a Jekyl and Hyde, to become the monster that might lurk just beneath the surface if the circumstances changed. When did all this end? Did it ever? She understood all right. Being with Bob had been like living in a terrorist siege for all those years. Never sure what would happen when, no matter how well she cooked or smiled or behaved, the unknown was always there. What would set him off this time? A slightly burned chop or a cold cup of tea? There must be hundreds of women out there, she thought, unable to leave for fear, lack of funds and nowhere to go anyway.

Her mind was made up.

They weren't all like Caroline. Savvy, smart and independent, determined to make a go of it on their own. Society accepted it and said nothing. That was the problem. She began to think about the Refuge in Sydney. What if there had been something like that for me and Danny? A safe house to go to? Hidden away somewhere safe and quiet, for women to escape to? Jenny needed a Caroline meeting over coffee. Definitely not a Bernadette one.

And if all this had never happened I would never be thinking this way. She smiled and relaxed into the dream. Something like hope seeded itself in her mind.

'Well, then,' she said out loud to the beach. 'I must have this job.'

That evening she found Megan and Evelyn. They had both approached her about their dangerous home situations, were both working that evening. She took them both aside in the Treatment room.

'Hey, girls. Could we meet up next week for a cuppa at my place? I've got a rather exciting idea I want to share with you.'

Intrigued, they set a time to meet up. She noticed that Evelyn the quieter of the two, had a very swollen eye. She said nothing, but a mix of anger and determination flooded her.

Sunday morning. Clouds scudded across the sun.

Jenny had retreated into a quiet reverie as Richard drove them down a tree-canopied road away from the beach. She had been relaxing on the lounge, writing lists of what she would like to have in a Women's Refuge. Such a brilliant new concept. Their actual own Bunjip Bay one. Well, somewhere nearby anyway. They could do it too.

Earlier that morning Richard had walked down the hallway shouting his usual halloooo, full of zest and smiles, and had persuaded her to come out for a drive.

'Let's go to the country just for a change. Might be nice to get out.'

Reluctantly, she went.

He leaned over while he was driving and patted her knee.

'What's up, Chickie? You don't look too good today. Is it your mum?'

Jennifer folded her arms and looked out at the passing countryside.

She sighed. 'No, not just that. You probably won't understand. It's just an idea I've got. Plus. I've, I've gone for a job.'

Richard withdrew his hand and looked at the road ahead.

'Oh. Well. That's great. What is it?'

Jenny began to unpack her dream. Hesitating at first, she gave him the sketchy outlines of what it might be like to provide safe housing for vulnerable women needing shelter, and her part in it. Richard turned the radio down and nodded. After driving in silence for a few minutes, he suddenly pulled the car off to the side of the road where there was a leafy clearing beside a creek. He stretched out his arms on the steering wheel and sighed deeply. He glanced over at Jenny, hunched in the seat.

'Well, I've got some news too.'

Jenny sat up quickly, opening the door as she did. Why am I so titchy all of a sudden? What's wrong with me?

With a smile, Richard launched into his news.

'I've been offered a franchise on a Health Food Café chain. It's the latest thing. Up at Bentley. I've got a week to make a decision on it. Thought I'd tell you today.'

Jenny flung herself out of the car narrowly missing a muddy puddle beside the car. 'I need some space,' she said.

She walked along beside the water trickling quietly through rushes and over stones. Coming to an old wooden bridge she decided to cross over to the field beyond. Finding a rickety wooden gate she leaned on it, gazing into gum trees and bush. Not a breath of wind stirred the leaves. She felt the peace settle around her like a mantle. She heard Richard's footsteps swishing through the long grass behind her. He put his arm around her and drew her into him, resting his chin on top of her head. She pulled away from him, looking away. Richard looked at her closed face. 'But I thought you'd be pleased.'

'Yeah. Sure. You're leaving. I knew it would happen. Everybody leaves. Eventually. Please take me home.'

An empty morgue of silence sat between them. Each of them enclosed by their own walls of misunderstood sentences. The landscape slipped by unnoticed, the trees waving as they passed.

When they arrived at Jenny's house, she slipped out without saying goodbye and slammed the car door hard. Richard sat in silence, hands on the wheel, looking for all the world like someone who had failed an exam he had studied hard to pass. He backed down the purple-flowered driveway and drove home.

Chapter 42

Caroline stood, arms folded, frowning. 'What do you mean you're not returning his calls? What has he done for Heaven's sake? Jen, you owe him an explanation.'

Caroline stirred her coffee in a mug big enough for a casserole. Jenny's coffee was still untouched as she sat opposite her friend in the café. Her face was a white mask of sad.

'It was only a matter of time, Caroline. This is how my life goes. Everyone I have ever been attached to leaves. In the end.'

'My God, Jen, you weren't this stricken when Bob died. Even when your Mum went.'

'Yeah. Well.'

Caroline looked at her friend, light landing. 'You really love this guy, don't you?'

Jenny pursed her lips together in a zippered line and folded her arms.

'Yep. Guess I do.'

Caroline leaned in over the table and grabbed her hands hard in both of hers.

'Jen. Go after him. Fight for this. Without being a drama queen, this is your pursuit of happiness. Don't just let it slide away.'

Jenny leaned back heavily with a groan, hands clasped on her head.

'I don't even know how. Anyway. Gotta go. I'll let you know if I get this new job. Now that's something worth fighting for.'

Later that night at work, Jenny settled all her patients for the long hours before daylight came again. Sleep was an elusive trickster, teasing with its promises of oblivion, fleeting as a shadow, as so many of them struggled to tie up the loose ends of a life finishing its tour.

She came into the Treatment room where she found Megan, her face pale in the fluoro glow of the glaring overhead light. 'See you next week love. I'm looking forward to it.'

'Yeah. Yeah. I'll just make sure it's OK with Gary and he doesn't need me for something.'

Jenny bit her response off before it arrived.

CHAPTER 43

Richard sat hunched in front of his wife's wardrobe, still bulging with clothes. The last bastion of remembered intimacy. Since Marilyn had died, he seemed to have lost his inner compass. Which way was north? Or even up? He had opened and almost shut the wardrobe doors so many times, and each time the flood of memories of twenty-five years of the ups and downs of marriage washed him away in its current and out to sea in a rip. He shook open the first of the many large plastic bags accumulated and ready for the job ahead. Brightly coloured dresses hung in precision representing a kaleidoscope of a life well lived.

Grief was a chameleon, taking on different shapes and colours according to what was being presented. It felt to Richard like a parallel universe, the other place he lived from time to time. It was the moat around the castle that secluded him from entering fully into life. Sometimes it presented itself on the if-only-I hadn't path, which wound itself round his heart like a tourniquet. To regret was to lose again.

Today was a quiet day, a settled day. He hadn't any idea why Jenny, the one bright shining light in his life for a moment, had cut him off so completely and irrevocably, and he felt like a severed limb in some ways. She obviously had second thoughts about him now. It had felt so much like the right time for change. Autumn rustled at the windows, scraping the panes with bare twigs. Time to recollect and re-sort his life. The offer of the franchise loomed like a rising sun, even though it was two hundred kilometres north of Bunjip. It felt like a fresh breeze blowing through the ash and cobwebs that had managed to accumulate in the three months since Jenny's sudden exit from his life. He felt not to barge his way back into her home but longed to know what in fact, he had done.

I thought we had something. Maybe not. If he was honest, he loved this woman. Thought the world of Danny. And as for Racquel coming into their lives ... cherry on the top.

Looking round the bedroom, his eyes fell on one of the last photos of him and his wife. They stood, arms around each other, champagne glasses raised, smiling up at the ceiling, toasting the future. Her red and blue Hibiscus shirt they got in Hawaii shouted joyously at the lens.

It had been a Surf Club do, lots of music and pizzaz and the usual mob, too much beer and way too loud. Neither of them knew about the cancer then. That came later. And then, life became about before or after the diagnosis.

He began to pull every item of clothing, dresses, cardigans, shirts and slacks, off the hangers, some still attached, and load up the green bags without looking too closely at anything, picking up pace, a frenzied madman in a dream. He left the shoes for another time. Something so intimate about shoes. The drawers still full of her clothes, her undies, her tops, would have to wait.

As if he might change his mind, he ran every bag quickly down the stairs and into the car, and without bothering to lock the house drove the fifty miles to the next town to the Op-shop drop off. They fell upon the bags like vultures.

Looking at the empty car and what felt like his very empty life, he drove to the nearest pub and downed two schooners too fast. Back in the car, he sat behind the wheel, feeling the tornado of emotions overtake him and spin him like a top. Glancing beside him he discovered one of Marilyn's shirts had been left behind on the seat. It was the one they got in Hawaii. The one in the happy photo. Almost afraid to touch this last vestige of memory he quickly grabbed it up and sank his face into the faint Red Door fragrance that had been Marilyn's favourite perfume. He let the tears come. Like a long-awaited release the flood gates of tears journeyed down his face, soaking the red and blue Hibiscus, as he breathed in her smell.

Finally he was spent.

The sun soaked into the asphalt of the pub car park, deserted in the middle of an ordinary working afternoon. He took a deep breath and rolled the shirt in a ball, stowing it under his seat. A new peace settled on him like a new day. With new resolve, he knew what he had to do.

Jenny's meeting with Megan and Evelyn had been hopeful and it had surprised her how full of creative ideas the other women were. What treasures lay buried under their survival mode. Who knew when one of them would need a refuge for the night? Or even longer?

Megan clasped her hands behind her head, leaning back into the lounge.

'We could rent a house somewhere. Maybe out in the country. Get the council to fund it.'

Jenny rolled her eyes. 'Yeah. That's going to happen, I don't think. But, yeah, I agree, great idea.'

Evelyn sat forward on her chair. She was the oldest of the three of them and her face was etched with a map of her life. She had worked on the Oncology Ward for over fifteen years. Her husband, Bruce was in and out of work all the time and was a bloke's bloke. But nobody wanted any part of him when the beer kicked in. Evelyn had borne the brunt of Bruce unleashed way too many times. She had two teenage kids and up 'til now had sailed through it all like a ship in a very long storm. Lately she had become twitchy and anxious and had missed a few days of work. Having a sick day here and there, and returning later in the week, looking at nobody and just filling in the hours.

She looked at Jenny and Megan. 'You know it'd have to be out of town, of course. People need to not be found. Sometimes ever.'

Jenny topped up their cups again out of the old teapot. 'Hmm. OK. Let's leave it where it is for now. By the way, girls, you do know you can always come to my place if ever you need a safe port in a storm, don't you? If this refuge is meant to be, it'll happen, right?'

Megan looked at the ground. 'Might be too late by then.'

CHAPTER 44

April and the merest chill crept under the curtains in Jenny's bedroom, the warning of cooler times. Dawn emerged, pastel and still as a pond. Sunday morning. Empty and silent. Jenny lay motionless in the cold bed, feeling a deep loneliness sweep over her like an arc from a lighthouse. With a groan, she threw back the covers and padded down the hallway. Danny was up already, scoffing cornflakes at the kitchen bench. All tousled haired and blondly innocent. She gave him a cuddle from behind and he patted her arm. 'Hi Mum. Surf's up today. Me and Jai are going to catch a few. Is that OK?'

'Course. Be careful. Watch the rips. Don't do anything stupid.'

He grinned at her. 'Would I?' He was off down the hallway and out the door. She waited for the click of the latch but knew he'd left it open.

Sun streamed in boldly filling every space in the kitchen. She carefully made her tea in the pot, thought of Hermione and how she loved proper leaf tea in a proper teapot. With a tea cosy if possible. Smiling at the memory and so grateful for what had seemed like borrowed time with her mum, she sat out on the veranda on the cane chairs where only days before she had met with the girls and talked about the possibilities. Maybe these things were only possible in the city. Who would fund a Women's Refuge?

Finishing her tea, she shoved her feet into her joggers and grabbed the car keys. Driving out along Casuarina Bay, she instinctively headed west towards the country road that she and Richard had travelled on that last day some three months ago now. The countryside was like a calendar shot, with cows grazing in pastures, rolling green hills and clumps of static stately gums standing proud. In the newness of a Sunday morning no cars came past. Autumn hovered at the edge.

Trees shed their leaves almost in reluctance as the season transitioned. A stand of Liquid Amber trees stood resolute and golden, on a small hill that looked for all the world just made for them.

She spotted the same place by the creek that Richard had pulled into that last day. Pigeons waddled about on the ground doing their rattly cooing like old women gossiping. She walked onto the rickety wooden bridge where a willow trailed its hair in the soft flowing water. Wandering across the bridge she was startled to see a path leading away from the bridge and a fairly old wooden gate set into a stone wall. The path wound up a gradual slope. The catch was rusted and immovable. Checking that no one was about, she climbed over the top and stood catching her breath, feeling like a naughty school girl trespassing.

Scribbly Gums towered above her, writing their stories up and down their trunks. They formed a cathedral of overhang blotting out the light which slanted through in shafts to the ground where she stood. She saw the grey tail of something slithering into the bush beside the track. The air was still and silent. A few butterflies crossed her path.

Crows began to gather in the trees above with their throaty ark-ark cries. The path was covered in vines hanging across and branches were beginning to creep across the space. It was not a well-trodden path at all and she could only just make out the direction it took.

She reached the top of the slope and looked down into a heavily treed valley. There in a clearing, barely visible was the tin roof of a house. With a sharp intake of breath she pulled back behind a tree. Nothing moved. The very air seemed to pause, waiting. A Willy Wagtail hopped in front of where she stood, quizzical. The distant hum of a plane could be heard in a cloudless sky as the sun climbed and warmed the space.

She ventured out and began to walk down the track also overgrown with Lantana with its acrid smelling pink and yellow blooms crowding out everything else in its take-over bid. Jenny did her best to deny all the what-ifs scrambling for attention in her mind. Thick bracken lashed her legs. As she got closer she could see a door wide open at the front of the house. The windows were all shuttered and on the ground was a shattering of broken glass. A lonely silence shrouded the whole site, settling like a mist of unknowing.

Looking up she saw that it had another storey built onto one end of the house. It had so many windows all around it that it looked like a cruise ship on a grass sea. It was a house of waiting. Her heart pounding, Jenny tiptoed around the corner to see the back section. A sudden flight of white Ibis beside the back door caused her to cry out as she watched their clumsy efforts to disappear.

The house was decidedly empty. She peered through the dusty cobwebs over the windows and could make out the outline of furniture, a fridge, cupboards. She looked around. Nothing moved in the silence but the lazy drone of cicadas came and went as the sun rose higher in the sky. The remains of a garden bed were visible under a huge overgrown passionfruit vine on a wooden trestle. A mango tree lurched forward at the edge of what had been a verge of grass and was now overgrown with weeds and vines. The decaying mangoes lay rotting on the ground, half eaten by bats. Decay and neglect hung in the air, waiting for a fresh breath. Jenny turned to face the road, suddenly aware of where she was and what she was doing. The hills around hid the house from view of any passing traffic.

'Perfect,' she said to herself as she made her way back to the car.

Life without Richard was now empty. It filled her with occasional longing and second thoughts.

'I'm alright on my own. Just me and Danny.' She convinced herself. Remembered that "to regret is to lose the battle a second time." Yes.

Danny sat at the kitchen table pulling the binding away from a book he was supposed to be reading.

'Mum. When are we seeing Richard again?' He looked up at his mum.

Jenny sighed. 'I dunno. Sorry, Darl. I know you liked him. Some things just don't work out. I miss him too.' She got up and filled the kettle.

Danny slammed the book shut. 'Well?'

She stirred her tea slowly and didn't answer. Danny scraped his chair back across the floor and ran down the hallway.

'I don't understand you, Mum. It's not fair,' he stomped down the hallway. The door slammed behind him.

The phone's strident ring brought her back to the moment.

'Yes? Jenny O'Hare speaking.'

The male voice at the end of the phone was honey smooth.

'Oh, hello there. This is Michael Smith from the Sydney Office of Family Resources. I am really happy to tell you the job is yours if you want it? We will be opening the new Office not far from where you're living so that should make it easy for you, too. '

With a sharp intake of breath Jenny answered. 'Wow. Yes please. I am really happy to say yes.'

'You'll have to come down to Sydney in, say, a week from now. We can give you the details of starting etc., then.'

This time it was tears of joy.

It was a couple of days later when she was able to get the girls together. A cold express train of a wind drove itself along The Esplanade, whipping the canvas awnings into a striped frenzy and scattering papers and rubbish across to the empty beach. Grey clouds gathered like angry faces and a few drops of warning rain fell.

Jenny met with Evelyn and Megan and told them in excited whispers about the house she had happened upon. 'It looks totally deserted. Maybe we can go and see the council about it?'

The other two women exchanged glances.

Chapter 44

'I've got some other news, too' said Jenny, widening her eyes. She told them about the new job and what it would entail.

CHAPTER 45

The three of them waited in the Council Offices in town. The walls were predictably cream and brown and the stuffy air locked itself into every crevice. The Queen looked down regally from her gilded frame alongside a list of town mayors back to the early 1930s. The only sound was a woman clattering away on a typewriter behind a glass screen.

The typing woman looked over the top of her glasses. 'Mr. Harris will see you shortly.' She resumed her typing, head down.

The door opened on their right. A thin wisp of a man with an apology of silver hair in random patches all over his head, appeared in the doorway. He looked way past retirement age and his lined face wore an expression of detached sadness like a head on a coin. Despair emanated from him. Silently he gestured for them to come in and quickly found a third chair from somewhere behind the office desk. He extended his hand to Jenny.

'Roland Harris. How can I help you ladies today? He sat down behind a desk that dwarfed him into insignificance. Even his chair was too low for him to adequately be in charge. He folded his hands in front of him on the desk.

Jenny began to tell him about the deserted house she had found in the bush and its approximate location. Evelyn and Megan nodded with quiet enthusiasm.

Roland Harris got up so quickly his office chair rolled on its wheels across the parquet floor and hit the wall. All three of them looked at each other with wide eyes. Without any explanation he went straight to a large metal filing cabinet and shuffled through the files.

'Ah. Here it is.' He said, pulling out an old manila folder full of papers. He placed it on the desk and rifled through the pages. 'I think you are talking about this.' With an almost theatrical gesture like pulling a rabbit from a hat, he presented a page of specifications and writing. 'There's a clearing on the left beside a creek. A bridge. You cross the bridge and go up a winding track that looks like it goes nowhere. But ... aha ... it leads to a little valley and here is a hidden house. And ... may I ask, why do you want to know?'

Jenny took the role of spokesman and glancing at Megan and Evelyn, she began to tell him about their plans for a safe refuge.

Roland Harris put his head on his chest and clasped his hands together. The three women prepared for a dismissal or at the least a patronising rebuttal. He looked up, and misty-eyed peered straight at Jenny.

He cleared his throat and pulled out a handkerchief to blow his nose. 'My daughter needs this. I'm at my wits end.'

He rubbed his eyes and sniffed hard. Taking a deep breath, he sat back in his chair. Clapping his hands together once he said, 'Right girls. Let's get down to business.' He turned a couple of pages over in the file. 'It's actually a deceased estate. Remember that head-on collision a couple of years back up on the highway near Casuarina? Them. Fairly young couple. No relatives to speak of. Been sitting there ever since. Just going to waste. This'd be perfect. My daughter ... well ... I guess you ladies may perhaps understand what I'm talking about here? There are times when, well, she needs a safe place to stay with the kids.'

They all nodded in agreement.

'Mr. Harris, we do know. My husband was the man who drowned on the Seven Mile a few years ago while he was fishing. Evelyn and Megan have their own story. There is a Women's Refuge in Sydney just opened and they are already overwhelmed with the numbers of women and kids needing a safe refuge. I've just been given a job through the Family Resource Centre. I've got the qual...'

He held up his hand in a halting gesture. 'Look, leave it with me. I reckon we can make this happen.'

He stood up and came out from behind the desk. Evelyn and Megan made for the door. Roland Harris extended his hand to Jenny and with some uncertainty, ignoring his outstretched hand, she put her arms around this very sad man and gave him a hug.

'Please feel free to give your daughter my phone number. I'd love to meet her and just encourage her.' Slightly taken aback, Roland Harris went back to his desk and fidgeted with the pens.

'I will do that. I'll be in touch. I don't need to tell you...'

Jenny shook her head and placed her fingers to her lips and smiled. 'Not a word, Mr. Harris, I've worked on an Oncology Ward for many years. People have told me secrets that I will take to my grave.'

He ushered them out and went back into his office, blowing his nose and quietly closing the door.

The three of them stood outside the Council building in the Autumn sun, smiling at each other.

Chapter 45

'Well', said Megan, 'Things are looking up. I've got chocolate cake at home. Yes?'

CHAPTER 46

Winter was at the edge of the sky. Waiting for an entry point.

It had been four months now since Jenny had spoken to Richard. Well, in any meaningful way at least. Their last conversation had been about her needing a break to think about things. Well, at least Jenny needing a break. Richard had put the phone down in bewilderment. Occasionally she had caught a glimpse of him, white overalls and truck, coasting along the Esplanade. She had run into a shop each time, to avoid any contact.

It was a Wednesday morning and rain had started to fall in thick ribbons from a darkening sky, filling the gutters to fast overflowing. A rumble of thunder shook its drums. She ran along the Esplanade and quickly turned the corner looking for a protective doorway. The rain stopped as fast as it had begun like an exclamation mark at the end of a sentence. She stepped out wet and bedraggled, walking briskly away from the heaving ocean and realised with a start that she was in Richard's street. Her clothes clung to her wet body like plastic and dripped onto the ground.

A large removal truck blocked the footpath. Suddenly he was there. Loaded with boxes and books that threatened to topple at any moment. Richard stood unmoving. Caught like the rabbit in the spotlight. Stunned, Richard dropped the box on the path. Books spilled everywhere over the wet ground.

Disregarding the mess he stepped towards her with the hesitation of the unknowing lover unsure of his ground and footing.

Jenny realised she was holding her breath and let it out like the hiss of steam. He was immediately in front of her. She let him take her in his arms as he buried his face in her damp hair.

'Oooh, I have so missed you, my darling.' She nodded into his shoulder, enjoying the sensation of being held in the deep place of arms around her. This was the place. An above and beyond knowing told her that right here and right now, this was where she belonged.

He stepped back from her for a moment then drew her into himself again with a groan. The kiss began gently like the very first time, then hungry and searching, reminding them how long it had been and how deeply they loved each other. The months, the weeks, the days fell away as nothing, right into this present moment of knowing, of being. Tasting and remembering the tenderness that had begun and ended too soon.

Jenny's tiny world was quite off its axis. Nothing more needed to be said. She knew what she hadn't known before.

A sudden crash beside them startled them apart. Two men in overalls had pushed a lounge chair up the ramp of the moving van where it had landed hard. The taller man, built like a heavy-weight wrestler wiped his brow with a hanky.

'Come on mate. Put that woman down. What do you want moved next?'

It was like waking from a dream. Another life was happening outside their moment.

Jenny took a step back. 'You, you're moving. Where?'

Ice came circling around her heart. She turned to go but Richard caught her by the shoulder.

'Look, Jen. This can wait. I was offered a franchise, a coffee shop one, up the road a few hundred k's away. But none of this matters. I, I just want to be with you. I'm not taking it.'

'Oh, Rich, I'm so, so sorry I didn't ring and...' He took her in his arms. 'We can work this out.' His lips made a line of determination as he stepped back from her. 'Can't we?'

She shrugged her shoulders and spread her hands, palms up in a surrender. 'Yes. Yes we can. I love you, Rich. I do love you.'

He dropped his arms to his sides. 'That's it. then.' Richard turned to the moving men.

'Sorry mate. I'm not going anywhere. I need you to put all this lot back. Sorry. I'm staying.'

The truckie rolled his eyes and crossed his arms. He stood with his legs apart in the way that particular men hold particular ground.

'You're kidding right? It'll cost ya.' And he began to laugh as he organised the other mover. He shook his head. 'Women!' he muttered.

And he began to unload Richard's life, putting it all on the pavement.

Jenny felt happiness in a way she had never experienced, coursing through her whole being, energising every fibre in her with life, like diamonds floating on a deep ocean without a wave in sight.

They stood looking at each other for a forever moment. Richard cupped her hand in both his and kissed the inside of her wrist. Jenny gave an apologetic smile.

'I'm sorry, Rich. It's just been ... I don't know...'

Richard put a finger to her lips.

'Later. Let's talk later. I've got a house to unpack.' He grinned at her and began to lift a box from the wet pavement. 'And it's going to rain again.'

'Oh, I've got so much to tell you. Come over tonight. I'm not working. Please?'

With a smile that went right through to her backbone, he turned back to the job at hand. 'I'll be there at six,' he said, and was already helping to unload the truck. 'Maybe a roast? With gravy?'

The rain had stopped completely and the sun punched holes through the grey rain clouds, reigning supreme. The town was washed and fresh. Jenny, drenched through, with rat-tail hair dripping ribbons of damp down her back, walked slowly towards the beach-front where people were beginning to venture out. A smile played around her mouth like a tune, and she felt a deep peace right to the core of her being.

The strange bird of hope had landed. Again.

CHAPTER 47

A roast seemed like the right choice for dinner. Jenny stirred the thickening gravy and checked the baked potatoes. Hair washed and shining and an ankle-length blue, cheesecloth dress set the mood. She foraged in the lounge room and found two unused vanilla scented candles, lighting them in their holders on the dining table. She twirled in the kitchen as Danny wandered in, dropping sand out of his jeans cuffs.

With a wide grin she turned to Danny. 'Guess who's coming for a roast dinner?'

Danny smiled like a Cheshire cat. He ran to her and wrapped his arms round her waist for a very long moment.

'That's great, Mum. Wondered what all the fuss was about. Got time for a shower?'

He ran off down the hall just as the knock came at the front door.

Richard stood in the doorway. Seeing him by the soft light of the street lamp across the road, in his pale blue jeans and a white shirt, she felt a surge of desire blaze like a sudden lit fire in very dry kindling. Her body tingled right to her toes. As he came down the hall she could see the large bunch of pale pink roses in his hand.

Danny ran out of the bathroom in his undies and wrapped his arms around a stunned Richard. He ruffled Danny's hair.

'G'day mate. Been too long, hey?' Danny nodded, then ran off back to the shower.

The baked dinner was just the right pick to cook. They moved out of the kitchen leaving the dishes for later. Richard leaned back across the lounge chair and gave a deeply satisfied groan.

'Oh my gosh, I have so missed your cooking. It's not really my strong point, is it?'

They sat close together, legs touching. The lingering smell of a baked dinner hung in the air. Danny fiddled with the new remote control changing channels at random intervals. Flick. Flick. Flick.

'So, you've got news too, Darl?'

Jenny took an unsteady breath then launched into all the news about her new job prospects.

'I've got the job if I want it. Starts after Christmas. They're thinking of setting up a Family Resource Centre up this way. Time to get out of nursing. And I've got the quals for it.'

Richard smiled and moved closer to her, taking her hand and giving it a squeeze.

'Yeah. No thanks to Bob. Well done, Chickie. You'd be so perfect for it too.'

'And, I need to tell you about a sort of deserted house I found. Remember that day we drove out into the country away from Bunjip?'

Richard looked blank. Then it dawned on him, 'Yeah. That was the last time I saw you.'

'I know. And I'm sorry I gave you nothing after that day. Anyway...'

Richard put his arm around her shoulders drawing her in close to him. 'Why did you run, Jen? I don't understand.'

She glanced at Danny, immersed in Bonanza. She took a deep breath.

'Look, I've thought a lot about this. I think I was just scared. Scared to give more of myself than I knew how to. Afraid of ... of, well, being loved I think. Probably doesn't make sense to you though, hey?'

She got up from the lounge and went out into the gathering night, out onto the back veranda. An evening breeze whispered secrets in the tops of the Sheoaks, humming agreement. An owl hooted in a nearby tree and then without a sound, she saw the flash of white as it took off. Richard followed her out.

'What is it? What do I have to do to show you I love you and you can rely on me?'

Jenny glanced sideways at him. 'You've done nothing wrong. Honest. I love you too. It's just, it's just that, well, everyone I get close to ends up leaving. One way or another.' She stood like a wooden doll, hands gripping the veranda rail. A cloud crossed the pale moon.

'Jen, you've going to have to trust me if we are going to go somewhere with this. I know it's a risk but look ... I reckon we can make it happen. Yeah?'

She turned to face him and smiling up at him, cupped his face in her hands.

'Yes. Yes please.'

'And stop running away from me.'

The sky was suddenly lighter. A perfect silver moon presented itself as if on cue, illuminating the entire veranda like a stage.

Looking up into his face she smiled the quiet smile of a woman in love. He bent down and kissed her. They heard the sound of the sliding door behind them.

'Bonanza's over. Just thought I'd tell you,' said Danny with a grin.

They drew apart and laughed, walking hand in hand back into the house. Richard put his arm round Danny's shoulders and gave him a squeeze. 'Righto, mate. We are right here.'

Danny closed the door behind them. And the moon shone down.

CHAPTER 48

The train from Sydney slid quietly into the station and doors clanged back. Racquel stepped onto the platform with her maroon case. Gone were the city clothes and stilettos. In her blue jeans and joggers with a white windcheater she still looked stunning. Jenny and Richard ran to meet her, and Richard took her bag. They moved into a huddle, laughing and full of news.

After lunch they walked on the Seven Mile. A pale winter sun peeped through banks of clouds. The sea swished quietly at the edges of the pebbly beach, behaving.

Jenny and Racquel walked arm in arm along the great sandy swathe, as grey sea grass billowed past them. A few gulls arced overhead in the leaden sky. Up ahead they could just make out the figures of Danny and Richard as they ran along the foreshore.

Jen stopped suddenly. Turning to Racquel she said, 'Would it be OK with you if, if I regarded you as the daughter I never had? I mean I know you've got a mum and everything, but... '

Without a moment's hesitation, Racquel hugged Jenny to her as tears welled up in her eyes.

'Yes, please. I would so love that.'

They stood together, looking out to the horizon.

Jenny squeezed her hand. 'I'm so glad we found each other.'

They heard the thudding steps of Richard and Danny as they raced back breathless along the shoreline.

Chapter 48

And Jenny felt a completeness she had never felt before.

THE END